Before It's Too Late

A Novel

By Joann Schissel

Literary Review

Published by Back Roads Literary Review
Knoxville, IA 50138

Copyright © 2024 Back Roads Literary Review, LLC.

All rights reserved. No part of this publication may be reproduced, distributed, or transmitted in any form or by any means, including photocopying, recording, or other electronic or mechanical methods, without the prior written permission of the publisher, except in the case of brief quotations embodied in critical reviews and certain other noncommercial uses permitted by copyright law. For permission requests, write to the publisher, addressed "Attention: Permissions Coordinator," at the address below.

ISBN 979-8-9884904-5-6 (pbk.)

Any references to historical events, real people, or real places are used fictitiously. Some of the places depicted are fictitious embellishments of actual places but beyond that, names, characters, and places are products of the author's imagination.

Printed by Ingram Spark, Inc., in the United States of America.
First printing edition 2024

Back Roads Literary Review
1699 Highway 14
Knoxville, IA 50138
www.backroadsliteraryreview.com

Acknowledgements

I'd like to thank everyone who made this debut novel possible including the members of the Marion County Writers Workshop who kept me inspired with thier critiques, advice, and encouragement. Also to my beta readers on Critique Circle and especially Elly and Jeanne from the local book club. Thank you to my brother, Joe, and wife, Paula for encouraging me to follow a creative path.

Most significantly, I want to thank the love of my life, Michael Van Natta, my husband, who without his encouragement, I would never have written fiction. From the first time we met when he asked me what kind of writing do I like, to his continuing wisdom and belief in me, I will always be blessed and grateful.

About the author

Joann Schissel lives with her husband, Michael Van Natta, on a vineyard in a small town in south-central Iowa, where they make wine and write books.

Chapter 1

San Francisco 2018

Melissa fidgeted in the plush chair of the psychologist's waiting area and past the time gazing out the floor-to-ceiling windows that framed the skyscrapers of San Francisco Bay. The morning fog had cleared away, but the gloomy light of the autumn afternoon lingered.

"The doctor will see you now," the receptionist said, ushering her into the consulting office that looked like a fabricated set staged for a photo shoot. Minimalist furnishings included two chairs, same as the waiting area, a mahogany desk and a table lamp covered with a green glass shade. A PhD diploma hung on the wall.

"How is your freelance work going?" Doctor Prescott asked after both settled into chairs across from each other. Round black spectacles made his eyes appear large, as if scrutinizing a specimen under a microscope. He brushed something from the sleeve of his suit jacket and opened his notebook.

"Work is not so great," Melissa said, fidgeting with her hands in her lap. "I lost a major account a few weeks ago. Madison Productions. The marketing manager said it was because of budget cuts, but I think it's because he didn't like my work."

"Why do you think that?"

She shrugged. "I don't know. I've been unfocused lately. The anxiety is getting worse. The other day I misplaced my laptop.

I always have it on the work desk in my apartment and I swear I had no recollection of where I put it. I found it in the laundry basket."

His eyebrows ticked upward. "Have you been taking any illegal drugs or using excessive amounts of alcohol?"

"Christ, no." She rolled her eyes. "Just those anti-anxiety herbal chews you recommended." She rubbed her manicured nails. "Sometimes I drink a glass of wine with food from the local deli at dinner. But that's about it."

He wrote something in his notebook. "Are you still managing your stress with walks in the neighborhood park?"

She nodded. "Yes, every day, like you told me to. And also, I tried volunteering at the animal shelter like you suggested. I thought being around animals would help, but it just made me more fearful. Afraid the dogs would bite."

Dr. Prescott placed his notebook on his lap. "So, diet and exercise could improve but it's within a normal range. You're a healthy weight, and frankly, an attractive and intelligent woman. How about your social life?"

She dug her nails into her palms and shook her head. "Actually, it sucks. I haven't had any meaningful relationships since my divorce. I can't get close to anyone. As soon as I start to like them or worse, fall in love, they run away."

"Leave you like your parents did."

She bristled with the remark. "Like my mother did, you mean. Dad was the one who stayed. The dependable one."

"Yes, your mother. Maybe we should try to explore that again."

Melissa shook her head. "I told you, Doctor. I prefer not to talk about her."

The doctor leaned back in the chair and interlaced his fingers across his chest. "Melissa, tell me what you want to accomplish here. We can't work on your problems if you refuse to face them."

Melissa grimaced. "I just want to resolve this feeling of dread, like something isn't right ... something missing and imbalanced."

"I can refer you to a physician who can provide anti-depressants if you want."

"No, I don't want to depend on prescriptions."

Dr. Prescott leaned forward. "It's common for many people at this time of their lives to seek to re-examine their circumstances. Mid-life crisis is real. Anxiety can leave one questioning the meaning of life."

Melissa took a deep breath and frowned. "I'm only 40 years old. I don't believe suddenly I'm having some kind of crisis. Frankly, Doctor, I feel like you're not helping me." She stood and gathered her purse, slinging the strap over her shoulder. "I appreciate your efforts, really, I do. But considering my financial situation along with my frustration with lack of progress, I think it's a good time to take a break from therapy."

***

Trudging up the three flights of stairs with mail in hand, Melissa unlocked the door to her apartment. On the wooden end table, envelopes stamped final notice mingled with printouts of resumes. A couple weeks after walking out of the doctor's office, her job hunt had failed to bring any good news. The meager amount in her savings would have to cover next month's expenses.

She browsed through the new stack of mail with hopes of a job offer. Instead, she pulled out a handwritten envelope postmarked from Iowa. An unfamiliar name of Gabe Murphy was printed across the return address.

Hesitant but curious, her fingers lifted the flap and removed the single sheet of stationery.

***

Oct. 4, 2018

Dear Melissa,

    I am writing to you because your mom is gravely ill and has been hospitalized. I beg you to set aside the past and come to Iowa before it's too late. She told me all about the history between you, and I just want you to know her situation and hope you will make the right decision. I'm sorry for the letter, but we didn't know how else to contact you. Please come as soon as you can. I will reimburse you for traveling expenses. My phone and email are below.

    - Gabe Murphy

    Frozen at her desk, she chewed her fingernail to a nub. Several years ago, Aunt Irene had called to tell her about her mom's remarriage to some Iowa farmer named Gabe, but she had shrugged off the news, not the least bit interested in Lydia's latest adventures.

    The letter triggered images of the last time she saw her mother in their driveway on that frigid spring day in Iowa. Wind had whipped strands of light brown hair across Lydia's tear-streaked face, the sight of her mother's distress chilling and turbulent as Melissa's bewilderment. She stood helpless to stop her as her mother shoved a suitcase into the car and drove away.

    Holding the letter from Gabe, Melissa paced into the kitchen re-reading its message. At least she had opened this one. There had been others, addressed with her mother's handwriting. Those had been promptly dispatched, unopened with "return to sender" scrawled on the front. The satisfaction of the act provided a much more powerful message than any reply.

    This sudden plea from a man she had never met made her skin prickle. Why concern herself about a selfish woman removed from her life for decades? The idea of returning to Iowa where she grew up reignited a knotted web of woolly nostalgia and dormant anger. What did this man, technically her stepfather, want from her? Why would he think this information could convince her to make a trip for someone who caused such bitterness? She held the letter for a moment. Curling her fingers around it, she crushed it in one swift movement, dropping it into the trash can.

That night, Melissa dreamed of wandering through a surreal landscape of luminous green grass and cartoonish flowers sprouting bright colors. Marshmallow clouds morphed into white doves and floated in a brilliant azure blue sky. Her mother and grandmother appeared beside her, conjured and shaped from adolescent memory.

Grandmother faded into the distance. Her mother's face came into focus, bright and smiling. Lips moved and radiated a shimmering tone. M-e-l-i-s-s-a. The sound of it stretched and hovered from far away.

The scene shifted in a flash, replaced with ferocious dark clouds, multiplying, and swirling into a furious storm. Lydia's face held a terrifying expression, exaggerated, and pulled into unnatural contortions. A giant vortex of wind and black dirt swept her mother into a deep abyss. Her elongated pink fingers reached out before dissolving into droplets.

The dream rattled her awake. The reverberating echo of her mother's voice calling her name faded into the hush of the night. She rolled over to check the alarm clock. The green digits glowed 1:23 AM. Closing her eyes, she replayed the scenes of the dream. Vivid, more than simply the impression of odd theater, its residue sparked an unexplained depth of emotional tugging and heartbreaking sadness. She lay awake, breathing deep to soothe the heaviness in her chest and the decision that weighed on her mind.

***

The next morning, she padded the few short steps from bedroom to kitchen to prepare her usual black coffee and dry, wheat toast.

She plopped her elbows on the counter, chin cupped in her hands and gazed out the solitary window.

The busy street three stories below filled the moment with mundane activities of the city. Cars rushed down the narrow hilly street at a frenzied pace only to be stymied at the red light. The blare of traffic seeped through the closed window with a familiar chorus of horns and sirens. A woman pushed a stroller along the sidewalk and stopped for a moment to adjust the infant's covering.

Turning away from the window, an object out of place caught her eye. A crumpled paper lay on the tiled floor.

Last night she swore the letter had been thrown inside the trash can. She retrieved it and flicked it back inside the receptacle, shoving it down with a determined punch. Done. Discarded. Just as she had been thrown away by her mother. An edge of the crushed paper quivered with a nearly imperceptible movement, like a rose blooming in slow motion.

How would it feel to never see her mother again? Never receive the satisfaction of an explanation and a deserved apology.

She reached for the wrinkled paper and smoothed it on the surface of the two-foot square dining table. The uncanny timing of the letter's arrival and the dream gnawed at her.

Perhaps the dream held some meaning in its vivid imagery and sense of urgency. Different than most dreams that are easily forgotten, this one stirred a feeling of raw emotion. A nagging itch that needed scratched.

Her eyes fixed on the letter. Grabbing her phone, she punched in several digits. After a few rings, a man's voice answered. "You've reached Gabe Murphy, please leave your message."

"Hello, Gabe, this is Melissa. I got your letter." She hesitated for a moment before speaking. "I'm coming to Iowa on the next available flight."

Chapter 2

Monday Morning

Sunrise blossomed over the runways of San Francisco International Airport the following morning. Melissa waited on standby, sitting in a hard plastic seat at the designated departure gate. Catching a flight to Iowa on this short notice had poor odds of success, despite the good fortune of snagging a buddy pass from a networking friend who worked for the airlines. Even that didn't guarantee a spot.

Her fingers tapped with impatience as the queue of passengers disappeared inside the jetway. Gathering her purse and a rolling carry-on bag, she stood, deciding her next move. A kernel of doubt nibbled at her. Abandon this trip that she didn't want to take in the first place, or press on?

A uniformed gate attendant behind the desk picked up a microphone.

"Melissa Streeter, paging passenger Melissa Streeter, please come to the United Airlines desk." Melissa blew out a breath and clambered toward the announcer.

"We just had a cancellation," the woman said. "This is your lucky day. It was the only seat left on today's flight to Denver, then on to Cedar Rapids." She printed out a boarding pass and handed it to Melissa.

Working her way through the narrow aisle of the Airbus, she found her row and squeezed past the man in the aisle seat occupied with intense study of a hefty novel. She settled in next to the window and removed her phone and an herbal anti-anxiety chew from her purse. Popping the gummy anti-anxiety chew in her mouth, she flicked through her emails and texts. No response yet from Gabe.

She looked up from her scrolling as another man sandwiched into the middle seat next to her. He had a thick head of salt and pepper hair neatly combed and was dressed in dark trousers with a long-sleeved polo shirt. Melissa guessed him at about fifty years old.

"Hello," he said nodding towards Melissa. "I almost missed the flight. A minute later and I'd be waiting until tomorrow to get to Denver."

She offered a slight smile and watched him stuff his carry-on bag underneath the seat in front of him. His arm brushed hers as he settled back and clicked the seatbelt. The scent of fresh pine drifted around him. She pressed her arm into her ribs and returned her attention to the phone.

"Are you headed to Denver, too?" he asked.

She looked up from her task. "Well, just the first part of the trip, I'm going on to Cedar Rapids."

"On vacation?"

Her face flushed with heat. She reached up to adjust the overhead airflow knob to maximum, attempting to formulate the briefest explanation possible. Blabbering about her troubles to strangers made her uncomfortable.

"No. My mother is ill…I'm going to visit her."

"I'm sorry to hear that, I hope she'll be okay." A genuine tone of sympathy resonated in his voice.

The amplified recitation of the flight attendant over the address system interrupted them. "Ladies and gentlemen, the captain has just informed us that our flight is delayed due to a squall over the Rockies."

A collective groan surfaced from the passengers. The flight

attendant continued with a soothing voice. "We will take off as soon as the captain receives permission from the tower to proceed. We apologize for the inconvenience and will get you to Denver as soon as safety allows."

Melissa touched her fingers to her forehead where sweat began to sprout. She swallowed hard, aware of the growing dryness in her mouth. Her heart beat faster.

The man observed her for a moment. "I've traveled a lot for work," he said. "This delay is not a big deal, it happens a lot with the weather. Everything will be fine."

"I've never much liked flying," Melissa admitted with a nervous smile, realizing he must have picked up on her troubled expression. She concentrated on slow breaths to quell the rising unease, shoving away images of crashing into a mountain.

Neither spoke for a few moments until he turned to her.

"My name is Jeremy." He held out his hand to shake hers. His grip felt firm yet comforting. His velvety voice exuded confidence.

"Nice to meet you, Jeremy. I'm Melissa." She studied his face for the first time.

His broad smile creased the laugh lines around his mouth and the corners of his intense dark eyes. A square, clean-shaven jawline sculpted his features with an angular impression.

Handsome. But in addition, he looked familiar, like someone she had seen in print somewhere.

"I'm headed to Denver for a genetics conference. I'm a researcher," he said.

"I'm a researcher, too, only in the marketing field," Melissa said. His direct and friendly nature intrigued her.

"You look familiar to me," Melissa said. "I think I may have attended a conference in San Francisco where you were a speaker."

"Yes, I've spoken at several conferences in the city. It's convenient for me since that's where I live."

Melissa's voice lifted in surprise. "Are you Jeremy Weaver?"

He pulled his head back in a slight tilt and his lips parted into a smile. "Why, yes, I am. You must have a very keen memory."

She smiled. "I heard you speak last spring about the analytics of population demographics."

"Did you attend that? What a coincidence that we're sitting here now."

"Yes, I was there. I thought your explanation of confirmation bias was very enlightening." She hoped her tone sounded professional and not too gushing with groupie-like admiration.

"Ah, yes, confirmation bias ... where we seek out only the information that aligns with our own values and beliefs, picking and choosing facts that bolster our position, ignoring any competing data." He smiled as if they had just shared an inside joke. "Did you have to travel from Cedar Rapids to attend that?"

"No, no, I live in San Francisco, too. I work from my home office, contracting with clients that need market research."

"Do you enjoy your work?" he asked.

"Yes, most of the time. I like solving problems with data. Kinda nerdy, I know, but it fits my personality."

He laughed. "I know what you mean, I'm that way myself. I wish we could solve all the world's problems using only undisputed facts, right? It would make life so nice and tidy. But just when we think we have everything figured out, our human nature intervenes and causes chaos."

Her intrigue about this man bolstered her gumption. "Does your wife travel with you to your conferences?" The thought slipped out of her mouth before she could stop it. She regretted the question the second his smile faded.

"No, I'm a widower. My wife died several years ago in a car crash."

A rush of embarrassment heated her cheeks. "I'm really very sorry."

"It's okay, don't feel bad." His voice turned wistful. "We had a wonderful marriage. Her passing showed me how fragile life is and can change in an instant. I took it for granted that we would grow old together."

"I'm so sorry for your loss," Melissa said in a hushed tone.

He nodded and turned his eyes downward. Several seconds passed before Melissa spoke. "Do you have children?"

His expression brightened. "Yes, my 2 adult children live in Oregon. I don't get to see them as often as I'd like. Work keeps me busy. What about you? Kids?"

She caught him glancing at her left hand.

"No. No kids." She hesitated then added. "I was married for a couple of years, but it didn't work out. We divorced about 8 years ago."

"I'm curious," he said, twisting a little closer to her. "I hope this doesn't seem too forward, but do you have Irish ancestry? You have a lovely combination of blue eyes and black hair."

Melissa blushed from the flirtatious compliment. She returned his smile. "Hmm, I've always thought Irish had red hair."

He nodded. "Yes, there is a common genetic trait for that which is why the stereotype persists, but there is also a small percentage with your complexion."

Melissa smoothed her hair back over her shoulder. Some people had asked her if she dyed it, which she had recently considered after finding a few strands of gray mixed in with her long, wavy curls.

"Well, my mom's family background was English, and my dad was Northern European, so maybe there was some Irish in there somewhere."

"What about family? Brothers or sisters?"

Melissa shook her head. "No, I'm an only child, raised in the suburbs of Des Moines."

"And your parents...they live in Cedar Rapids?"

"Well, yes and no. My mother and her husband live there, or around there, somewhere in the country." Her answer came out stilted. She didn't want to delve into an extended explanation about her parents and felt relieved when the droning of the aircraft engine hummed louder. The plane rolled back from the gate, interrupting their conversation. A wave of pleased murmurs rose from the passengers.

"Ladies and gentlemen," the flight attendant's voice chirped, "the tower has given us the go-ahead for takeoff. Please make sure your seat belts are fastened and all carry-on items are stowed."

Once they were in the air, time rushed by. They chatted about work, favorite restaurants, Bay Area museums, earthquakes, and current events. He had an easy conversational style that she liked, straightforward, humorous, and thoughtful. Melissa didn't recall a discussion with a stranger this enjoyable in a long time.

When the flight attendant rolled the beverage cart through the aisle and stopped next to them, they both looked up.

"What can I get you?" The flight attendant asked Melissa.

"A ginger ale would be great, please."

"I'll have the same," Jeremy added. The flight attendant poured the sodas and held one of the cups toward Melissa.

"I can pass it to her," he offered, accepting it from the attendant and turned to Melissa. She reached over to take the cup. Their fingers touched for a second, then lingered a second longer. Melissa sensed a spark, a sliver of energy running from her fingertip, fleeting and ephemeral. He smiled, turned back to retrieve his cup, and held it toward her in the air in the fashion of a toast. She followed his gesture, and they touched the paper cups together. "Here's to lucky coincidences and good fortunes, he said with a grin."

They had just finished their beverages when a melodic tone sounded, and the seat belt alert light flickered on the overhead display. "Good afternoon, this is your pilot. We are expecting a bit of choppy air on our descent into Denver. Please make sure your seat belt is fastened. We'll be touching down shortly."

Within minutes the smooth trip transitioned into something that felt like racing over a series of speed bumps on a freeway, followed by a jolting yo-yo on an elastic string. Melissa pressed into her seat and gripped the armrest. She swallowed the urge to reach for the paper bag tucked into the seat pocket in front of her to deposit the contents of her stomach. When the plane tossed up and down then side-to-side, she grabbed Jeremy's arm out of instinct to hold onto something.

When the craft pitched again, he leaned in close to her, his voice low and calm. "This is why they call Colorado the Bronco state." Melissa blew out the breath she held with a squeaky laugh.

Once safely on the ground inside the terminal, Jeremy reached into his pocket, pulled out his business card, and handed it to her.

She nodded and took the card. "Thank you, Jeremy. You certainly made the trip a lot better for me."

His eyebrows raised. "I'd love to have yours, too."

"Oh, yes, of course." Melissa dug into her purse, produced the card, and handed it to him.

"It was nice chatting with you, Melissa, I hope we can share danger again sometime soon." He flashed a charming smile. "Oh, I hope your mom gets better, too."

For a moment their eyes locked as if neither wanted to look away. And then she watched him turn and stride through the buzzing crowd of travelers. Flirtatious men typically struck her as annoying and easily dismissed, but Jeremy made an impression. She slid his card into a small pocket of her purse.

***

The weather unfolded clear and bright on the second leg of the journey across the Midwestern plains. A million notions swirled in her mind as she sunk into her compact seat. Closing her eyes, she allowed her thoughts to wander, combing through the myriad of questions. A few days ago, her life had been a joyless routine. Meeting Jeremy sparked an unexpected interest. He seemed interested too. His easy-going manner and intellect occupied space for daydreams, even though the possibilities of any future courtship seemed remote.

Romantic relationships had failed her in the past. Marrying had been a huge mistake. It didn't take her long to discover her ex-husband's drinking mixed with anger issues forced her to end the marriage. The smattering of dates she had in the last year panned out into a pit of disappointment. Men she had met through work always proved to be too self-centered or banal. What held the key to true love? Did her mother ever love her father? And whatever motivated her mom to marry a farmer years later, after the divorce?

Gabe held mystery, too. Her mother's husband. Dairy farmer. Stepfather. Those labels held all the knowledge she possessed about him.

She fidgeted in her seat and peered out the portal window. The flat ground below painted geometric sections of greens and amber. Sparse threads of roads wove around distant structures dotting the landscape. Returning to Iowa sent a wave of unsettled nostalgia through her. The thought of reconnecting with her estranged and now-ailing mother spurred a stew of consternation peppered with wariness.

The plane touched down in Cedar Rapids late in the afternoon and she reached for her phone on arrival. A message from Gabe appeared in her inbox.

> Will meet you at the airport to pick you up. I'll be holding a sign with your name. I have some bad news.

Chapter 3

Monday

Melissa departed the plane and scanned the public waiting area for Gabe. The cavernous room held an array of people busy looking at phones or the overhead display of arrivals. Squeals of greetings from embracing families echoed around her. No one held a sign like Gabe had instructed her to watch for on arrival. It occurred to her that she had no clue what he looked like, only a vague idea of a man in his sixties.

Her thoughts swirled with nervous anticipation. Somewhere in the crowd a stranger knew more about her than she cared to share. A man who assumed the role of a family member. Must she trust someone merely because he held a sign with her name? Pushing aside the nagging trepidation, she chided herself for not asking to swap photos of each other through email.

Rounding a corner of the terminal, she spotted a tall man standing alone, away from the smattering of cheerful travelers and loved ones reuniting with hugs and energetic voices. Slivers of gray hair peeked out from under his green ball cap. His long-sleeved plaid shirt tucked neatly into jeans cinched with a belt around his thick midsection. Stout fingers clasped a ragged piece of cardboard with Melissa's handwritten name.

She slowed and held her gaze on him. He adjusted his wire-framed eyeglasses and stared back at her, raising his eyebrows.

"Melissa?" he asked as she approached. His face held a somber expression, puffy eyes rimmed with pink.

"Gabe?"

He tucked the cardboard under his left arm and extended his right hand in greeting. "It's nice to finally meet you," he said grasping her hand. "Do you have any luggage?"

"No," Melissa replied. "Just this carry-on."

He nodded. "I reckon you're wonderin' about your mom." His dark gray eyebrows lowered. "Let's head outside and talk in the truck."

Melissa followed him outside to the parking lot where Gabe pointed to a dust-coated pickup truck. The rust around the wheel wells and the dents in the vehicle's body spoke of hard work and rough times. Gabe opened the squeaky passenger door and loaded her bag inside the truck cab behind the seat. He held the door open for her as she pulled herself into the cabin onto the battered leather seat. The odor of cow manure and sweat escaped. Her new designer sneakers crunched the dried leaves on the floor and brown dust clung to the light-colored canvas shoes like a magnet.

Gabe circled around the truck and clambered onto the driver seat but didn't start the engine.

"Sorry for picking you up in the work truck, but the sedan is in the shop in Decorah."

"It's quite alright," she responded in a polite tone and looked at him with intensity. "How's Mom?"

Gabe removed his cap, brushing a hand through his hair in one swift movement before interlacing his fingers and resting them between his knees. He turned toward her, pressing his lips tight, eyebrows lowered. She stared back into his blue eyes that began to glisten with tears.

"Melissa, I'm so sorry." His wrinkled face compressed into a frown. "Your mom passed away this morning."

***

Low steel-gray clouds filled the darkening sky and the air chilled as they drove to a small wood-framed building on the outskirts of town. A flickering neon sign in the restaurant's window displayed The Driftless Diner. The small gravel parking lot hosted a semi-truck and two pickups.

"I need some coffee for the drive home," Gabe said.

He pulled opened the glass door of the diner for Melissa. "I suspect you may be hungry from your travel. I haven't eaten today, and I need something in my stomach. It's a far piece to get back home."

She trailed beside him, her steps dragged, robotic and weary. The possibility of her mother's death had crossed her mind, but she tamped it down. Part of her wanted an apology. But there would be no last words from her mother, contrite or otherwise. No unanswered questions satisfied. Images of her previous night's dream rushed back with all its foreboding shadows. The shock of the news left her emotionally barren, hardened into a frozen outward reaction. Heaviness grew in her chest but a lightness in her head caused a sense of being twisted and pulled apart like taffy. Despite her growling stomach, she had only a paltry appetite.

The smell of fried chicken filled the air of the diner. "Maybe a bite of food would do us both some good right now," Gabe said.

They seated themselves into one of the booths lined along a row of large windows overlooking the highway. Dim interior illumination, punctuated by pendant lights, hung over the retro-styled table and vinyl-clad seating. Piped-in music played a mournful blues tune in the background that absorbed the hushed conversations of the few, mostly male customers, hunched over plates of food, chewing in glum motions.

She held the laminated menu, browsing the meal descriptions with a mechanical sweep. A waitress appeared, placing a couple water-filled glasses on the table.

"Howdy," Gabe said in a tired voice to the woman. "I'd sure like to get one of those loose-meat sandwiches and some strong coffee, please."

The unsmiling server jotted something on her note pad and turned to Melissa. "Whata you have, Hon?" she asked, pen poised above the order pad.

Nothing on the menu appealed to Melissa. "Do you have anything vegetarian, maybe some hummus on gluten-free pita bread?"

The server cocked her head of bristled brown hair and replied with a sigh, "We have a grilled cheese sandwich on white – comes with fries."

Melissa cringed, recalling the heavy, greasy dishes she once consumed as a teenager. She had become accustomed to the sophisticated, lighter fare of the West Coast.

"Sure, I'll take that." She closed the menu, resigned to the selection, one the first of many dietary compromises anticipated in the next few days.

The waitress scribbled a note and disappeared into the kitchen.

Gabe folded his hands on the table. Puffy eyelids behind his glasses created a haggard appearance, like a man who had weathered many storms. Despite his drained look, something unspecified about him comforted her. Perhaps his demeanor or the tone of his voice that held a tenderness, a steadfast spirit.

"I'm really glad you decided to come," Gabe said, shooting a glance at her before blinking away. His eyes fixed on the water glass.

Melissa read the anguish on his face. "I'm sure this has been rough on you."

A brief urge to reach for his hand washed over her, but instead her arms hung heavy by her side. Her sentiment felt more like consoling a stranger on the death of his wife instead of the significance of the passing of her mother. She cried for days after her grandmother died, but that same outpouring of grief evaded her now. Only a dull sensation coursed through her. To move past this week as soon as possible and get back home.

BEFORE IT'S TOO LATE

Gabe shook his head. "I still can't believe it. He paused and took a slow breath. "The doctors said it was from a broken blood vessel, a brain aneurism. At first, they were optimistic she would recover, but all they could promise was a wait-and-see. That's when I wrote the letter to you, not knowing if you would come, but believing you might." He looked up at her.

"Of course, I wanted to come. I'm so thankful I got your letter." She shifted her weight, admonishing herself for the discrepancy of truth.

"What happened...when she died?"

His eyes lowered. "I was by her bed in the hospital for the three days she held on. By the beginning of the third day, the doctors didn't hold much hope for any recovery."

Gabe made a slight nod and cleared his throat. "When the end came, I was dozing in the chair next to her bed, close enough to touch her." He fell silent for a moment. "Then something strange happened." His eyes glistened.

Melissa leaned in closer. "What? What happened?"

"I heard her whisper I love you. So sweetly. Just like in those moments before we kiss goodnight. I swear it was clear as day. I jumped up next to her, expecting her to be awake, but...she wasn't. She looked just like she was asleep."

Melissa shivered. Obviously, he must have been dreaming. She understood how dreams could seem real.

His index finger rubbed his eye behind his glasses, and he shook his head. "I remember alarms goin' off and hearing code blue blarin' over the PA. A bunch of people in scrubs rushed in and surrounded her. I stood back out of the way and heard a monotone sound. Then I saw the flat line on the monitor." His voice cracked and he took a long drink of water. He retrieved a handkerchief from his pocket, swiping it under his nose.

She imagined the moment of death and the timing of her evocative dream. A mere coincidence, yet an involuntary shudder ran through her.

The waitress reappeared, placed the meals in front of them, performed a quick sweep of their faces and hunkered away without comment. A wafting aroma of steaming food sparked Melissa's hunger. Her gaze lingered on the toasted sandwich and golden fries that made her mouth water.

Gabe looked at his plate, took a few bites and picked at the crumbled beef with a fork, rearranging the meat that spilled outside the bun. "I usually gobble these sandwiches right up, but I'm not feelin' that hungry now," he said.

Melissa chewed her sandwich, swallowing it along with the tightness in her throat. The week ahead would not be pleasant.

Chapter 4

Monday Evening

"Is there anyone you want to call to let them know about your mom?" Gabe asked after they left the restaurant and were back on the road. "I mean, your dad or someone?"

The faint glow from the truck's dashboard lit his face with a subtle greenish phosphorescence as they rolled down the highway. Melissa shook her head and raised her voice louder to be heard over the hum of the vehicle's engine. "Dad is living with his third wife in Northern Italy. I doubt he'd care."

The minute she uttered the statement, she winced at how harsh it sounded. "Sorry, Gabe, I didn't intend to be insensitive. It's just that he was very bitter over her leaving and never really came to grips with it."

"I understand," Gabe said. "What about a friend or relative?"

"Well, I was thinking about calling Christy, my friend from high school. She still lives in Des Moines and we've kept in contact online. As far as relatives, it's just my Uncle Pete and his wife, Irene, but they're elderly now. They live somewhere in Florida."

"I recall your mom mentioned Irene at one time to me, but I don't know anything about her."

Melissa frowned. "We never heard much from either of them after the divorce, even though Pete and Dad are brothers. They disapproved of what happened in the family ... the divorce. Dad blamed my mother for Pete's snub. He said it was because she brought shame to the family."

Gabe's jaw clenched and he tightened his grip on the steering wheel. She anticipated he wanted to say something but if he did, it remained unspoken.

He looked out the driver's side window for a moment before turning toward her. "Well, I suspect the funeral will be Wednesday or Thursday if you want to invite anyone. I'll make arrangements tomorrow with the funeral home."

They both fell silent. Light rain spotted the windshield and the rhythmic slap of the wipers lulled Melissa into her thoughts. Country music played on the radio with a mournful tune. A growing spiral of regret about this trip nagged her. She wished she hadn't committed to coming, and now an entire week in this dreary place loomed ahead of her. Chewing her lip, the thought of the unpleasant ritual of a funeral and all that entailed sparked a desire to get a return flight tomorrow. Get the hell out. No one could stop her if she wanted to leave.

Gabe broke the silence. "I know this probably wasn't an easy decision for you to come, Melissa, but I'm happy you decided to be here. That took courage."

He seemed to read her mind. Gabe appeared to be a nice enough guy, tolerable anyway. His comment needled her sense of obligation. Pressure to fulfill expected responsibilities. Did her mother think about these same principles when Melissa needed her?

She procrastinated the decision, weighed down by doubt. Leaning her head back, she gazed out at the night that hung like black velvet, mesmerized by the rain. The yellowed illumination from the passing town's streetlights strobed across the windshield. Raindrops on the glass sparkled in a momentary release before the byway once again transitioned into long, dark stretches of the two-lane. She imagined the road ceased to be a highway, but instead a funnel into the past.

"Gabe, how did you meet my mom?" Her voice sounded

drowsy.

He took a slow inhale and smiled. "We met in high school. She was the most beautiful girl I'd ever seen and was always beautiful to me until the day she died."

The openness of his romantic sentiment surprised her. "I didn't realize you two had known each other then." Melissa recalled whenever her mother began a sentence with when I was in high school, it guaranteed a tuning out.

"I don't remember her talking much about her high school years. How long did you date?"

"Throughout our senior year. Went to prom and graduated together."

"When did you break up?"

He took a long breath before answering. "Both of us kind of knew deep down that summer after graduation things would change. I enrolled in the agriculture program at Iowa State in Ames that following fall. She decided to stay in Des Moines and live at home with your Grandma Ruth. We didn't see each other much after that."

"Did you ever talk about getting married?"

"We talked about it, like most teenagers in love. But she wanted to study art, maybe go to New York City. Certainly not become a farm wife. I wanted to learn about agronomy and animal husbandry and work with my uncle on his dairy farm."

"I can't see Mom choosing a rural life. Well, not while I knew her anyway." She digested the thought for a moment. "Although, thinking back, the subject of her art always seemed to be old barns and country landscapes."

Gabe nodded. "I was devastated when we broke up."

"Hmm, that's when she met my dad. She was a student at the community college where Dad worked construction. He had already graduated college."

Gabe nodded. "Well, according to the story Lydia told me, Ruth convinced her that Robert would be the best choice of a husband. Ruth liked Robert because he had a college degree in engineering and business. Plus, he had a good job with potential. I guess he impressed her with his charm."

"That's odd. As a kid, I saw their actions as indifferent...like they didn't seem very fond of each other. Grandma and Dad rarely spoke -- or even smiled -- when the family got together."

"I reckon early on Ruth saw him as the better provider. Figured he could give Lydia a good life. More than what a dirt-poor farmer could offer. I suspect economics played a role for your grandma since she had her own money struggles after your grandpa passed away. She probably thought a wealthy husband for her only child was the answer."

Melissa pictured her grandma, puttering around in the kitchen, always baking something sweet and aromatic. A vision of the perfect 1950s housewife with her starched apron and hair neatly wound into a bun.

"I spent a lot of time with Grandma after school while Mom worked. I was 12 years old when she died." A memory popped into her thoughts of sitting next to Grandma, reading a book to her. "I remember she talked to me about marrying well long before I understood what that meant. I thought it was like the fairy tales about the prince and the princess that lived happily ever after." Melissa shook her head, scoffing at her own childish notion. "It's so sad that women in Grandma's time thought they needed a man to take care of them."

She turned to Gabe. "So, when did you and my mom finally reconnect?"

"We met again at our thirtieth high school reunion. We were both single then. It's odd, neither one of us had gone to a reunion until that one. We recognized each other immediately, just like old times. Before you knew it, we were dating again and married a couple years later. Our marriage has been the best years of my life. Hers too, I think." He cleared his throat and pulled a handkerchief from his pocket to wipe his eyes.

Melissa imagined her mother dating. "It's amazing that you hadn't seen each other in so many years and still felt the same attraction."

"Well," Gabe hesitated. "We did run into each other unexpectedly once at the Iowa State Fair one year. It was shortly after she was married. She volunteered in the cultural arts building and I was showing some cows. I spotted her and your grandma inside the cattle barn admiring one of my calves."

"I remembered going to the fair with her every August," Melissa chuckled. "As a child, I wondered why she always wanted to go to the cattle barn. It became a tradition. I thought she just really liked cows. We would sit on the bench outside the barn in the shady area and eat ice cream she bought from the dairy store inside."

Gabe grinned, "Yeah, the August heat always seemed to be blast-furnace-hot, so you'd have to gobble up the ice cream before it melted."

She smiled at their shared fair-time experience. "Yes, I remember that. I liked the cheese curds too. She always got a package to take home."

"Remind me to give you some of the curds we make so you'll have something to take home, again," he said, tossing her a smile.

The truck slowed and shuddered, turning onto a bumpy surface. "We're almost there," Gabe announced. Melissa stretched upright, relieved. Her body ached from the day of travel. The truck's headlights lit up the road in front of them. Gravel crunched beneath the tires as they drove into the driveway.

She opened the truck door and slipped out. The rural area at night felt like being in outer space. So, unlike the familiar omnipresent lights of San Francisco. Evening cloaked the surroundings with inky blackness outlining the shape of the two-story farmhouse in front of them. Clouds had dissipated and stars glittered in the dark sky. The curved sliver of the waxing moon glowed with a brilliance that dominated the broad expanse.

Gabe dropped her carry-on bag beside him on the floor as they entered the house and flicked on the foyer lights. A loud bark pierced the air and a blurred ball of tan fur rushed toward them. Melissa braced herself for an attack. A large dog greeted Gabe, dancing in circles, tail wagging at high speed.

"Hi, Doc." Gabe hunched over and rubbed the muscular panting animal between his floppy ears. Melissa stepped back, recalling a previous encounter with a snarling dog at the animal shelter.

"He's friendly, he won't hurt you." Gabe smiled. "Doc, sit," Gabe commanded. The dog obeyed, mouth opened, pink tongue hanging loose and wet, quivering with each excited breath.

"I'm just not accustomed to dogs, especially big ones," Melissa said, targeting the animal's face and retreating another step away. Doc's round eyes returned her stare.

"What kind of dog is he?"

"Mostly golden retriever with a mix of lab, maybe. Lydia got him at the pound when he was a few months old."

"That's strange," Melissa said. "I always thought Mom never liked dogs. That's why we didn't have pets. Dad told me it was because she didn't want animals in the house."

Gabe cocked his head. "Well, I can tell you she loved Doc. The two of them spent a lot of time together," he said. His smile turned doleful as he scratched the dog's bushy neck.

Melissa pointed toward her bag. "I can take that now."

"Oh, yes," Gabe snapped his head up. "We have a guest room down the hall. Follow me."

He led her through a hallway lined with small, framed paintings of barns and cows. The dog followed.

The modest guest bedroom included a double bed with a patchwork quilt and a side table with a lamp tucked next to it. Gabe switched on the lamp. The light cast a pale blue glow across the room.

"There's a bathroom right around the corner." Gabe gestured

in the direction. "I hope this is okay for you."

She placed her bag near the closet door. "It's lovely, thank you. Frankly, right now, I'm so tired, a halfway decent couch would be welcomed."

"Is there anything else you need?" he asked.

"No, I'm fine. Thanks, Gabe, I'll see you in the morning,"

He turned to leave. The dog hovered next to him studying Melissa with ears pointed forward.

"Yes, goodnight, get some rest and we'll talk more tomorrow," Gabe said, issuing the dog out and closing the door.

She ran her fingers along the puffy quilt, bright with a jumble of colors and patterns, pulling it back. Leaving her suitcase untouched, she dropped onto the bed, peeling off her yoga pants and sweater. Her undershirt would suffice as a nightgown for tonight. Slipping underneath the covers, she inhaled deeply, snuggling into the bed. The faint scent of lavender from the sheets triggered a vision of her mom scrubbing the entire house in cleaners with floral fragrances, obsessed with housework.

Melissa rolled to her side and closed her eyes. Hovering just before sleep, she visualized her mother in the kitchen. Melissa stood at hip level beside her.

"Make your bed, Melissa, before we go." Her mother's voice wavered echoey and distant. "You have to get ready."

Melissa looked upward at her mother wiping the countertop.

"Ready for what, Mama?" she asked in a child's voice.

"You have to get ready for what's coming."

Her mother's voice faded away.

Chapter 5

Tuesday Morning

Melissa awoke to a rooster's crow in the distance, just as her room brightened with morning light. She folded the pillow over her ears and tried to go back to sleep, hoping the rooster thing wouldn't be a daily occurrence. Slivers of daylight penetrated around the edges of the curtains creating patterns of luminescence flitting across her face. She yawned and sat upright, surveying the bedroom, grounding herself in the unfamiliar space. Her phone showed 9:00, only 7:00 West Coast time. No wonder she felt groggy.

Silence permeated the house, no traffic noise from vehicles rushing to their destinations, no honking horns, no sirens that began a typical start to her day in the city. A sleepy thought occurred to her about where the nearest Starbucks would be found until she realized a triple vanilla latte was probably not likely this week.

The quest for morning coffee beckoned Melissa to find the kitchen. She slipped on a pair of designer jeans retrieved from her bag, a long-sleeved t-shirt and sneakers and sauntered down the hall. The house appeared larger to her than it did last night in the dark. At one time it must have been a traditional style, two-story farmhouse, remodeled now with the interior designed in a contemporary-country motif.

She stood in the entryway by the front door listening for

sounds of Gabe or the dog, but the house remained hushed as if she had stepped into a church.

The sunlit foyer extended upward to the full two stories of the house. A large octagon window positioned near the top of the clerestory architecture where the high wall and ceiling met, held a view of the sky. The window framed wispy clouds floating in a background of robin-egg blue, giving the impression of an incidental piece of kinetic art.

She peeked out the sidelight windows that flanked the door to the bright day. Adjacent to the door, a lavender sweatshirt hung on a coat rack. A pair of pink house slippers were tucked neatly in the corner on the tiled entryway. The items must have belonged to her mother. Tangible tokens of the woman who lived here just days ago. She brushed the sleeve of the soft fabric for a moment before turning away.

Melissa sauntered around the central staircase, through the formal dining room, and strolled into the kitchen in the rear of the house. A handwritten note rested next to the coffee maker on the speckled marble countertop. Help yourself to coffee and food, I'll be back later this morning.

Sipping her brew and chewing a piece of stale muffin, she gazed out the sliding glass door in the kitchen that led to the deck. Doc reposed on the grass, penned inside a large dog run enclosure in the yard. His head rested between outstretched legs.

The view beyond the yard expanded to a wide vista of gently rolling hills surrounded by even taller stony cliffs. Beyond a row of dwarf pine trees and shrubbery rose a metal roofline, probably a barn, gauging by the cupola and weathervane. The abundant landscape of tall grass and remnants of late-blooming prairie flowers delivered an expansive vista. So different from San Francisco where every square inch of space packs a myriad collection of urban habitation.

Despite being born and raised in a state known for agriculture, she had not spent any time in the rural environment. Her childhood home had been in a city suburb. Neighborhoods, roadways, and sidewalks existed on flat, level ground, ordered in predictable simplicity.

A clammer rattled her from her thoughts. The ringtone of a classic old phone rang out somewhere within the house. Her phone lay in plain sight on the countertop. The ringing had not originated there. She held her breath, following the sound as the volume amplified near the stairway. The steps creaked below her feet as she ascended the stairs to the upper level. Three doors lined the hallway, one door opened to Gabe's room, and the other opened to a bathroom. The ringing persisted behind the closed door at the end of the hall. She stared at the door debating an urge to snoop inside, perhaps answer the caller. Stepping forward, she grasped the doorknob. It didn't turn. The ringing stopped. She dropped her hand to her side, questioning why an interior door would be locked.

Returning downstairs, she grabbed her phone from the kitchen and walked into the living room. Shelves bordered the walls filled with hardback books on French impressionism, agriculture, business, and cooking. Books written by Carl Jung and Viktor Frankl looked familiar from her college days in psych class. Small decorations occupied the space between volumes. A detailed figurine of a Holstein cow with a calf beside her; a ruby red glass shoe that held a few round peppermint candies inside the cavity of the heel; and a kitschy ceramic Leprechaun painted with a comic grin sitting on a stone.

She plopped on the couch in the living room and scrolled through emails on her phone. A message from her landlord reminding her about the rent. Yet another rejection message from a company where she had sent her resume.

Her phone buzzed with a text message.

> Hi Melissa, it's Jeremy Weaver. You know, from the Denver flight? Hope I'm not intruding on your family time. Would you be

interested in meeting for coffee or a drink after you get back? LMK.

She pictured his pleasant smile. How much did she trust him? After all, their encounter lasted the length of a plane ride. True, he intrigued her, but she had her share of worries to deal with now. The gamble of a new relationship only added complications to her life. Still, she couldn't help but grin.

Chucking the phone onto the coffee table, she rose from the couch and paced the room, surveying her new surroundings.

Several small, framed photo portraits were arranged on the mantle of the fireplace. Family pictures in the homes of acquaintances and friends had never really interested her. They merely represented unfamiliar smiling faces documenting events and places that held no meaning to her. But these photos kindled her curiosity.

She picked up a photograph of her mother and Gabe, posed in the typical head and shoulder position used by family photo studios. Probably taken before the time of mobile phone apps. Gabe showed just a speckling of gray streaking throughout his black hair. Her mother reflected a family resemblance to Grandma Ruth. Shoulder-length hair, peppered with a blend of light brown and gray draped her face. Eyes and jowls sagged a bit even though her smile spread wide. Was her expression genuine? Melissa remembered her as dour and melancholy. Was her mother so much happier living without a thought about her own daughter? She shoved the picture back on the shelf.

Few family photographs existed from Melissa's childhood. The one of her mom and dad on their wedding day, along with pictures of her as an infant had disappeared. Most of the collection had vanished, missing after she left for college. The keepsakes had likely been destroyed. Her father claimed the photographs had been accidentally misplaced in the upheaval of relocating to other residences after the divorce. Whatever the circumstances, she had little desire to reminisce about it or mourn the loss. She just never put much thought into it. Until now.

Another, smaller picture attracted her attention. Something seemed familiar about it. She grasped the frame and brought it closer. The Polaroid snapshot looked worn and faded. An artifact from a generation ago. Two young people stood close together smiling at the camera. The boy wore an ill-fitting tux and the girl a blue chiffon floor-length gown. A single white carnation corsage graced her wrist. The frilly background decoration constructed with crepe paper and balloons laced across an archway with a sign that read Class of 1973. She recognized her mother as a teenager. The resemblance of the young man's appearance struck her as unmistakable. The same symmetrical square face, broad grin and shaggy, black hair pegged him. Her date must have been Gabe.

A pleasant memory surfaced of sitting next to Grandma Ruth flipping pages of a photo album. She must have been around 10 years old when saw this same picture. Ruth wove some tale about it but left out the name of her mother's companion. Melissa had never asked about the boy and focused on her mother instead. The floor-length, empire-waisted gown; hair curled on top of her head with light brown tendrils coiffed to meticulous perfection. Lydia graced the scene like a fairytale princess. The only thing missing was a tiara.

She placed the picture back on the shelf when the kitchen door squeaked open.

Chapter 6

Robert and Lydia 1975

"Get cleaned up, Lydia," Robert said. "We're going to Dave and Susan's house tonight."

His announcement took Lydia by surprise. "Who?" she asked, rolling the vacuum cleaner into the hallway closet.

"Christ, Lydia, get your head out of the clouds." Robert's face pinched. "Don't you remember I told you about Dave? We work together on the project management team. I'm training him since I'm the senior foreman. He invited us over for drinks at their house tonight. Go get ready."

She brushed a loose strand of hair away from her perspiring forehead. Although tired from the housework, a chance to socialize with another couple excited her. She missed the few girlfriends she used to have. Robert didn't like her hanging around with single women, so her friendships had drifted away. He had told her that now she was married, she had to focus on her husband and domestic life.

She picked out the nicest pair of bell-bottom jeans and held up her favorite blouse for scrutiny. The blouse fit a little tight after she accidentally washed it in hot water, but the flower pattern was still bright. She liked the way the scooped neckline and sheer sleeves cuffed at the wrist made her feel pretty. The bodice hugged her small waist and emphasized her bust. Robert would be pleased.

When they arrived at the bungalow in Beaverdale, a young woman greeted them with a friendly grin at the front door.

"Hi, I'm Susan, come on in."

Inside the living room, a wood-burning fireplace toasted the cozy space with the smell of applewood. A macrame holder woven with course sisal hung suspended by the window and cradled a pot of sparse green ivy.

After polite introductions, the men settled into chairs by the fireplace and the women headed to the kitchen together.

Susan brushed her long hair over her shoulder and turned to Lydia. "What do you want to drink?"

"I'll just take a 7-up or Coke."

Susan smiled. "You don't have to be of legal drinking age here, you can have something stronger," she said pointing to a bottle of rum.

Lydia giggled. "I'll be 21 in a couple months. I just don't like the taste of alcohol."

"I guessed you were a teenager," Susan said, taking a long look at her. "Robert looks a little older than you."

"Yes," Lydia said. "About 10 years."

Susan raised an eyebrow, handing her a can of Coke. "How long you been married?"

"Just about a year. How about you?" Lydia snapped the top off the soda with a burst of fizz.

"Been a couple years for us. We got married right after college. You're a lucky lady," Susan said. "Robert's a handsome man. Dave says he's a hard worker, too, probably on his way toward upper management."

Lydia smiled. "Yes, he's very smart. When we got married, he told me I never had to worry about earning a living, because he'd always take care of me. So, I quit school after a year at community college and we got married. He was my Prince Charming."

Susan drew her head back. "Take care of you? You know we are living in a new time of the women's liberation movement, right?

Women must have freedom to do what we want, including jobs."

Lydia's eyes widened. "Oh, yes, I mean, I have a job. I'm a temp office worker, you know, for different companies when someone goes on vacation. I do typing, filing, answering phones, that sort of stuff."

Susan's lips pressed together, and her eyes rolled away from Lydia. She placed two cans of beer and her rum cola on a tray. "Can you bring in the plate of cheese crackers, please?" She motioned toward the living room. "Come on in and have a seat."

The women joined their husbands in the cozy room, situating themselves onto a well-worn couch. Robert and Dave faced them, seated on frayed upholstered chairs, chatting about football scores. Lydia surveyed the room. Her eyes settled on a display of a series of framed charcoal drawings that graced the scuffed, painted walls. One featured a bowl of fruit with a half-eaten apple, another showed a figure of an unclothed woman reclining among flowers. Others of various sizes portrayed every day, common objects.

She studied the portrait of the nude woman. "These drawings are wonderful."

Dave grinned. "Thanks, I drew those. Do you have an interest in art?"

Lydia nodded. "Yes, I took art classes all through high school. I love to draw and paint."

Dave leaned forward. "I belong to a group of artists that meet weekly. Everyone takes turns hosting at their house. We draw or paint still life or portraits, stuff like that. If you're interested, you can join us. We meet every Thursday at 7:00 in the evening."

Lydia grinned at Dave. "Yes, that would be great. I'd love to, thank you! I've missed my art classes and would love to learn from other artists." She glanced at Robert. He scowled at her with a clenched jaw.

"Well, I'll have to check the calendar when we get home to be sure." Lydia looked away and gulped her soft drink.

***

The ride home held a suffocating silence. Robert's hands gripped the steering wheel like a vice. His face seethed a mix of anger and suppression.

Lydia squashed the urge to speak until she couldn't stand the silence any longer. "I'd like to go to that art group that Dave talked about," she said in a timid voice.

"Now Lydia," Robert's stern tenor hissed in a low tone, "you know you can't do that. That's the time when you need to be home to make dinner. That's our time together in the evening. I don't see how traipsing off to some party would be appropriate." A grimace crossed his face. "Besides, I saw how you looked at Dave tonight. The way you flirted with him. I'm not letting you anywhere near him."

"Robert, I don't understand why you think that." She tried to recall what she did to deserve his stinging accusation. "I was just excited about doing something with art. It wasn't about Dave." She waited for his response. Her chin quivered.

Robert's posture stiffened and he threw a sideways glance at her chest. "For Christ's sake, Lydia, don't wear that shirt again. Makes you look like a whore."

His words stabbed her like broken glass. Her stomach churned. She faced away from him and leaned her head against the car window, fighting back tears. Once he made up his mind about something, there was no changing it.

After Robert snored in bed later that night, she carried her nightgown into the bathroom and hung it on the doorknob. Lathering with soap, she scrubbed her cheeks with vigor, determined to wash away the hurt. Hot tears and cold water mixed into a froth.

She tore off her favorite blouse, crumpled it, and pushed it into the bottom of the trash can. Somehow, she had to work harder to please Robert.

Chapter 7

Tuesday Morning

"Hello!" Gabe called out as he entered the kitchen from the back door.

Melissa walked into the kitchen to greet him and studied his face. "Good morning."

His face sagged. The wrinkled dress shirt was partially tucked under his belt. Everything about him looked tired. He removed his ball cap and raked his fingers through his hair. "I've been at Wilson's funeral home making the arrangements. I had an early appointment there and didn't want to wake you."

"I thought you were probably doing farm chores."

"Oh, I don't do the bulk of the farm chores anymore," he said, pouring a cup of coffee and sitting at the kitchen table. "Well, unless something needs my attention. My hired workers do the milking and feeding. At my age, I don't know how I'd run the place without them."

He grasped the cup and looked at Melissa with a somber expression.

"The funeral is set for Thursday. Visitation is tomorrow evening. I hope that works for you."

Melissa brought the coffee mug to her mouth and took a long, slow drink. A nagging urge to escape all the unpleasantness of ceremonial rituals drove a desire to hasten her return home. The original intention of the trip had died along with her mother.

Answers to questions destined to remain unresolved. Her emotion-filled dream from the previous night in San Francisco proved to just be like any other. Nonsense. Nothing profound or revelatory. Yet its message brought her here.

She stumbled with her response. "Well, uh, I need to revisit my schedule."

His face drooped and he looked at the rim of the coffee cup with puffy, red eyes.

"Let me check it right now," She reached for her phone.

The flight back had been scheduled for Sunday morning but perhaps could be changed to something earlier. Gabe, wrapped in polite concern, unwittingly offered an easy out. She could use an excuse on the premise of workload. Too busy to stay that long. Instead of pulling up her calendar, she punched in the airline website and waited for the flight information to load.

She looked at Gabe. His sagging shoulders and disheveled appearance reminded her of the homeless man who, on occasion, would huddle on the sidewalk near her apartment building. He'd remain fixed in the spot, dressed in ragged clothes layered on his diminutive frame. His only movement was a raised, cupped hand bearing fingerless gloves. Those who hurried by him avoided his presence as if he didn't exist. She felt sorry for him and would often slip him a few dollars, sometimes a sandwich. His eyes would lift for a moment, glistening with tears.

Melissa checked the screen for departures. Seats were still available for tomorrow's flight to San Francisco. Her finger hovered over the book-now button for a moment. Biting her lip, she withdrew her hand. Gabe's expression looked so pitiful. She placed the phone on the table. "Looks like my schedule is clear."

His face brightened. "That's good news," he said and pushed his chair away from the table.

She offered a weak smile.

"You know, the farm was special to Lydia. I wonder if you'd like to take a quick tour around? You ever been on a farm before?"

"No, not on a farm like this. The closest I've come to real agriculture is a vineyard in Napa Valley."

Gabe rose from his chair and rinsed his coffee cup in the sink. "Well, it probably won't be as glamorous as Napa Valley, but hopefully you'll find it interesting."

He looked down at her feet. "Those sure are nice slippers. Did you bring some ... uh ... sturdier shoes?"

Melissa looked at her designer sneakers and understood his point. "No, just my everyday shoes ... guess I never thought I'd need ...." She stopped and watched Gabe take a few steps toward a closet and reach inside. He pulled out a pair of ankle-high boots, colored a putrid green with a thick rubberized material that wrapped around the chunky toe and heel. Brown, dried mud crusted the soles and around the sides. They smelled like gym socks.

He held them in his hands for a moment, then thrust them toward Melissa.

"Here – we call these muckers because they're good for walking in the muck."

She wrinkled her nose and clasped the tops with a pinch between thumb and forefinger.

"These were your mom's. Maybe they'll fit."

***

Melissa trudged a few paces behind Gabe through the yard, past the dog pen. Doc snoozed within the enclosure under the shade of a nearby tree. She picked her way across the roughened, grassy terrain, managing to sidestep the occasional pile of dark bio-deposit left by some unknown animal. The boots cramped her toes with a tight grip.

Gabe stopped at the yard's perimeter and shaded his eyes with a flattened hand, squinting at the pale blue-gray sky. She caught up with him and brushed her palm across her perspiring forehead. The air carried an organic smell of dirt and straw. Her skin erupted in dewy droplets. "Ugh, I'd forgotten how humid Iowa is."

"Yup, the weather is hotter than a day in October should be," he said.

"Is it much further?" Melissa said, thinking about sipping iced tea under a shady patio.

Gabe motioned in the direction of the barn. "Not far at all. I think you might like seeing the calves first."

They crossed the fence through the gate. Sparse, weathered gravel littered the surface of the foot-worn trail flanked by short trees. The path eventually opened onto a broad expanse of short prairie grass. Just beyond that lay a smattering of old buildings.

Gabe led the way toward a rough-hewn building made of wood. Heavy posts anchored the corners and beams held the corrugated metal shed roof. A wooden railing surrounded the structure. Melissa trailed close behind him, slowing her pace to take in the surroundings.

The barnyard bustled with activity. Workers in jeans and baseball caps scurried between outbuildings or operated farm machinery. Cats skittered to-and-fro in different states of excitement. A kitten popped its head out between the gaps of the railing, making a hasty retreat to hide when Melissa neared it. A large rooster plodded toward her, its rangy legs propelled jerky movements. He strutted close enough to cock his head and fix a beady eye on her. Elevating his neck upward, he unleashed a shrill cackle. Melissa took a step backward. "Will it bite?" She cut a wide berth from the creature and edged closer to Gabe.

"Probably not, but it's best you don't get too close. That's Henry. He's just showing off for the hens. He keeps the tick population down, likes to eat 'em." Gabe cracked a grin.

"Ticks?" Melissa repeated, scratching her upper arms.

"Yeah, they've been pesky this year. It's a good idea to do a body check for the rascals before you go to bed."

Melissa imagined the feel of bugs crawling on her and worse yet, separating one of the bloodsuckers from her body.

They walked together toward a group of calves housed under the shed.

"The calves live in these pens, called hutches, for about three months," Gabe said.

Two weeks old and already the size of Great Danes, their bodies formed a mosaic row of black and white patterns. Melissa lingered close to a calf and peered into its wide-set eyes. The side of the baby's broad head sprouted fuzzy, oval-shaped ears where a yellow plastic name tag dangled like a pierced earring.

"Hello, Winnie," Melissa said, reading the name tag.

The calf's pale tongue protruded over one side of her mouth, creating a cartoonish expression.

"Where are the mother cows?" Melissa asked.

"Mom and baby stay together just long enough for the calf to get the good colostrum for immunity. Then they are separated shortly after birth."

Melissa frowned. "That seems cruel. Why do you do that?"

"It may sound cruel but actually is the best course of action, done for a lot of reasons," Gabe said. "One reason is the mother-baby bond forms within a day or two. If that happens it's a lot harder on them when weaning time comes. Both bellow night and day. You can hear their sadness by the tone of their cry as they search for each other."

"What do they do for food? Do they eat grass?"

"They are bottle-fed until they are old enough to eat. Baby learns to rely on humans for all her needs. Winnie never knew her mother and Mama hardly knew what the hell happened. Their connection never develops."

Winnie lifted her pink nose and produced a loud m-o-o. Melissa shrank back, startled by the volume of the youngster's deep bellow.

"It's ironic," Melissa said.

"What is?" Gabe raised his eyebrows, pushing his glasses against the bridge of his nose.

"The cow's sole purpose in life is to provide milk from her body to satisfy hungry humans, yet she never has a chance to nourish her own offspring."

They watched the youngsters for several minutes without speaking.

"Gabe, can I ask you a personal question?"

He looked at her, eyebrows raised. "Of course."

"Were you ever married before my mom?"

He tightened his jaw. His weathered hands dangled loose from the railing, and he nodded. "Her name was Beth. Married 10 years. I was a widower when I met your mom." He gazed out in the distance.

A melodious ring chimed from his jacket. Retrieving the phone from his pocket and checking the call number, he said, "Mosey over to the main barn." He motioned in the direction with a slight tilt of his head. "I'll catch up with you in a few minutes."

Melissa turned and walked toward the main barn, a large, wood-framed building a few yards distant. The sunshine had swept away, erasing the sharp morning shadows, and cooling the air. She scuffed her feet across the ground – a mix of dirt, mud, and the occasional pile of various animal droppings. The increasing breeze carried a scent of dried manure, not quite as unpleasant as she expected.

Inside the barn, about a dozen cows lined up, side-by-side in a row by feed troughs the size of bathtubs. A wide-slatted wood fence corralled the herd. One by one each animal jutted her head out over the rail, eyes surveying the stranger. They stretched their necks toward her in unison, raising their noses with nostrils widening. Ears twitched back and forth.

A vague feeling of being judged by the group of large beasts crossed her mind. Melissa studied them, impressed by their massive presence, yet non-threatening and curious demeanor. Large, pink udders ballooned like engorged bags ready to rupture at any moment. The cows soon returned to their feed, jaws sawed in a lazy side-to-side rhythm as if she no longer held their interest.

Gabe interrupted her thoughts as he entered the barn. "That was Angela. She's coming from Florida for the funeral."

"Who is Angela?" The name wasn't familiar to Melissa.

"She's your mom's best friend, probably the only person that knows her as much, maybe more, than me. You might want to meet her."

Before she could respond, raised voices from distant workers barked out in alarm. Gabe and Melissa hurried out to the barnyard, greeted by sudden northwest wind.

His attention turned skyward with a concerned expression. "Clouds movin' in."

Melissa followed his line of sight skyward. Marine blue clouds merged in tight formation on the horizon. A defined separation between the bleached sky and darkened mass coalesced like a giant ocean wave approaching a shoreline in slow motion.

"That's what I feared," he said. "Hot and cold crashin' together in one place makes for a hell of a storm."

A frigid chill danced around her, and thunder rumbled. The breeze she welcomed just thirty minutes ago, energized. Her hair swept into a frenzy, stinging her face.

"Storm's coming," Gabe said looking at her, eyes intense. His hand gripped her upper arm. "I've got to batten down the hatches here and make sure the workers get to the storm cellar. Best you head on back to the house now. Go to the basement." His instructions sounded deliberate and calm, but his face carried worry.

"What about you?" Melissa's voice rose in urgency.

"Go now!" he said, sprinting away from her.

Melissa scurried past the vacant area where the kittens had played earlier. Gusts of wind pushed her off-balance as she quickened her pace toward the house. It appeared small and far away. Shifting daylight diminished to an ethereal, greenish hue. Lightning flashed from the approaching clouds.

She broke into a run across the field of prairie grass. An empty feed bucket tossed in the wind overhead, nearly striking her. It hammered a beat as it crashed to the ground behind her with a hollow thud. The taste of silty dust filled her nose and mouth as she reached the yard.

Rain pelted her with a wet gush as she neared the house. A loud crack fractured the air. She squinted, searching for the source. The sound originated in front of her, near the dog's pen. "Doc!" She shouted over the noise of the tempest. The burgeoning wail of a distant tornado siren quelled her cry.

The dog's head emerged momentarily from the doghouse, eyes wide in fear. He retreated and disappeared inside. A thick, partially severed branch hung vertically by a tenuous sliver above the shelter and swung in the wind like a wayward pendulum.

Another splintered limb hurled toward Melissa, and she plunged face down into the dirt. The debris whirled past her. Just as she lifted her head, the swinging branch plummeted onto the doghouse.

Chapter 8

Tuesday Mid-morning

Melissa raced toward Doc. Reaching the dog pen, she heaved the gate open and clambered inside the fenced area, shielding her face against the blowing rain stinging her eyes. Debris peppered the ground. The fallen limb filled the enclosure, its thickest part extended horizontally on the roof of the doghouse. Although branches had crushed the top, it stopped short of falling all the way through.

She battled her way toward where Doc cowered, shoving the fractured limbs away. It took every ounce of strength to budge the obstructions aside. Her muscles screamed with each exertion. Frenzied wind pummeled with relentless fury, jostling her against the splintered tree bark that tore at her arms and hands. Rain lashed at her face and chest like icy pinpricks as she maneuvered the smaller branches to clear a path to Doc. She neared the doghouse and caught a glimpse of Doc hiding deep inside.

The frightened dog inched forward to the opening of his shelter, blinking against the wind. His body trembled. She crouched down and reached out toward him. "Come on, Doc, don't be scared." Her voice steadied to reassure not only the dog, but herself. He lowered his head and didn't move.

Gabe shouted somewhere behind her. "Doc, come!"

The dog raised his ears and propelled toward Gabe in one swift leap, squeezing past Melissa, nearly knocking her to the ground.

Gabe careened toward them, waving his arm in a wide arc motioning toward the house. "Quick, get inside!"

Melissa dodged tangled rubble as she worked her way out to Gabe's outstretched hand. He grabbed her wrist. All three of them tumbled through the back door and rushed down the stairs to the basement.

Once inside with the door shut, the roar of the wind quieted.

"Are you okay?" Gabe asked in a breathless voice. He pointed to the blood trickling in a slow stream down her arm. "Looks like you're hurt." He grabbed a towel off a nearby shelf. "Hold this tight against the cut. I'll get something to clean the wound." He turned and disappeared into a small bathroom.

Concentrating on slowing her rapid heartbeat, she toweled off and pressed the damp terrycloth against her oozing injury with a shaky hand. Wet clothes clung to her, and she shivered.

Doc shook and twisted his body, spraying droplets everywhere. Melissa cupped her hand over her nose to minimize the smell of wet dog hair. He watched her for a moment before plopping down on his haunches and scratched his ear with his hind foot.

Gabe returned with a first aid kit. "This may sting a little," he said. He wiped something that smelled like antiseptic on her wound. She winced from the sting.

"It doesn't look too bad. Not cut you got a hell of a scrape there." He stuck a large bandage over the reddened abrasion. Turning toward the couch, he seized a wadded-up blanket. "This will warm you up," he said, draping the tattered bedcover around her shoulders.

"But you're drenched, too."

"I'm fine. I'll dry off with another towel in the bathroom. Be right back."

She crumpled onto the couch and scanned the room. An assortment of vintage furniture and shelves lined the gray block walls. A beat-up wooden dining table sat near the center of the chilled room supported a stack of cardboard storage boxes. Bare lightbulbs overhead lit the space and chased shadows to the corners of the walls.

Gabe returned with a towel around his neck, his gray hair sticking out in all directions giving him a frazzled look. He turned to Doc, bending close to the animal's face, and ran his hand along Doc's back. "He looks okay, not even a scratch." Gabe seated himself in a wing chair adjacent to the couch. Doc hunkered down on a rug beside him.

"Good thing you got to him when you did," Gabe said.

Melissa shook her head. "He was too scared to come to me, so I wasn't much help."

"Who knows if that doghouse would have held together? You cleared a path for him to get out. You could have just run by him to get into the basement, but you stopped to help him. That was a brave thing."

She shrugged but secretly glowed from his compliment. "I didn't stop to think about it, I just knew I had to help him."

"That's something Lydia would do — run toward danger to save an animal," he said in a soft voice, rubbing Doc's head. He chuckled. "One time last winter, a pickup with a snow blade was plowing a foot of snow on the road here by the house. The truck slid all around on the ice, a couple times almost driving into the ditch. One of the farm cats ran across the road and got caught in between the mounds. Right in the truck's path. It didn't help that the cat was white, too. The driver probably didn't even see it." He continued petting Doc's head. His face took on a faraway expression.

She waited for a few seconds. The wind rattled the narrow basement window. "So, what happened?"

Gabe shook his head. "That dumb cat just disappeared in the snow. Lydia watched from the window. She ran out the front door and hightailed it through the drifts to fetch him. Probably saved it from gettin' flattened. She didn't think about herself getting run over by the truck."

Melissa sank back into the couch cushion, picturing her mother thrashing about in the wintry mess. A story most likely an embellished recollection. She wrapped the blanket tighter around her. The scrape on her arm began to ache. "How long do you think we have to stay here?"

"I suspect the storm will pass before you know it." He rested his hands on Doc's back.

Water droplets plopped somewhere from an unseen leak. Melissa sighed and picked at a loose thread on the arm of the couch.

"Tell you what," Gabe said. "Ask me a question about anything you want. Then I'll ask you. Honest answers only."

Melissa considered the suggestion for a moment. The game may be a good way to know him better. "Okay, I'll start."

Gabe nodded.

"You said you were married before my mom. Did you have any children?"

"No." He lowered his chin. "I was young when I married Beth. We wanted a family. When we found out she was pregnant, we were over the moon about it. She wanted to be a mother so badly."

Gabe hunched his shoulders and rubbed his forehead. "Beth had two miscarriages before finally the third pregnancy looked good. She was in her third trimester when the accident happened." His voice wavered.

Melissa regretted the simple question that obviously poked an uncomfortable memory. Her mouth dropped open to apologize, but the unformed words stuck in her throat.

Gabe leaned forward, interlacing his fingers on his lap. "Beth was driving alone that night coming back from the grocery store." He paused for a moment and took a deep breath. "Her car was t-boned at an intersection. Semi-truck ran a stop sign. She died in the hospital shortly after arrival. The baby couldn't be saved either. A girl."

Melissa gulped hard, biting her lip. "Oh, my god, Gabe, I'm so sorry. I didn't know."

Gabe straightened upright and slipped off his glasses, wiping the lens with the corner of the towel. He sniffed and repositioned the glasses over his nose.

"Your turn," he said lifting his chin. "Do you have kids?"

Melissa shook her head. "I never wanted to be a mom. Didn't have that desire, unlike a lot of my friends. Like Christy. She obsessed about having a baby and talked about it even when we were just in high school. I focused on my career. My husband didn't care about kids anyway. Of course, we were only married less than two years."

Gabe cocked his head. "What happened? If you don't mind me asking. Just didn't work out?"

Melissa snorted out a breath. "Well, when I had to explain the bruises on my face to friends and clients, I knew something had to change."

Gabe's eyes widened. "Did he beat you?"

Melissa frowned. "The abuse started slowly at first. He'd get crabby, then mean. Pretty soon he started lashing out at anything that made him mad. Pushing me against a wall, slapping my face, stuff like that. I never had broken bones, but I knew the physical part would only get worse. So, one day I packed his suitcase and put it on the curb. I changed the locks. There was no way I was going to put up with that." She shrugged at the memory. "I think he was glad to go, anyway."

Gabe shook his head. "No woman should have to suffer from abuse, of any kind, physical or emotional, period."

The wind began to ease, and the rattling outside quieted. A glimmer of sunlight emerged through the small windows at the ground level above them.

"Looks like it's passed," Gabe said.

Melissa looked at him. "You owe me."

"What do you mean?" He asked, turning toward her.

"You answered one question, I answered three." She smiled. I'll need more answers from you."

Chapter 9

Tuesday Afternoon

The rain stopped. Gabe and Melissa climbed the stairs from the basement.

"I'll check out the damage," Gabe said, reaching the back door.

"I'm getting out of these damp clothes," Melissa said and darted to her room. She returned to the kitchen with a fresh sweater and jeans. Gabe worked outside, kicking at debris, and holding a chainsaw.

Leaves and small branches lay strewn in disarray, cluttering the yard, yet the farmhouse stood unharmed. Doc's shelter did not fare as well. A foot-wide tree branch rested on the crushed roof, its longest branch just barely missing the backyard deck.

She made a cup of hot tea and listened to the mechanized whine of blades chewing through wood. Gabe finished slicing a large chunk of tree and Melissa called to him from the doorway. "Do you want anything? I can make some tea."

He straightened up with a labored breath and adjusted the safety glasses that reached across his face.

"What?" He said removing his earplugs.

She stepped outside onto the deck.

"Tea." She shouted and held the cup with an outstretched hand. He shook his head. "No, thanks."

"Need any help?" Melissa hoped her offer would be turned

down, wanting instead to take a break from farm adventures.

"I'll let you know, but I can get this cleared up myself without too much trouble."

Melissa surveyed the wreckage strewn everywhere with raised eyebrows.

"I've got some scrap lumber and shingles from a roofing project so the doghouse can be fixed," Gabe said.

His confidence struck her as a mix of reassurance and underestimation.

A wet snort erupted behind her. Doc stood in the doorway with his floppy ears picked up.

"Doc should stay inside the house for now," Gabe said, reinserting the earplugs.

She turned to Doc and pointed a finger at him. "You're a lucky dog."

Lined markings surrounding his mouth fashioned an expression of what looked like a smile.

Melissa ambled back through the kitchen into the living room and plopped on the couch. Finishing her tea, she ran through a mental checklist of tasks to accomplish. Keeping busy with something would distract her from the creeping melancholy mood. Her eyes drew toward the family portrait on the shelf. Lydia's stare etched unflinching back at her. Melissa broke the gaze and picked up her phone. She punched in Christy's number from her phone contacts. Connecting with her best friend from high school would provide some relief. Besides, she wanted to tell her the news.

"Hey, Christy, this is Melissa."

Her friend's cheerful voice on the phone soothed her with familiarity. Always the optimist, Christy's exuberant personality and chattiness differed from Melissa's tendency toward sarcasm and introspection. In school, when Melissa studied alone in the library, Christy would likely be at some social event or cheerleading practice.

"Oh my God, Missy, I haven't heard from you for the longest ... what's up, everything okay?"

"Well, not really, I'm in Iowa now." Melissa winced. "I have some bad news." She hesitated to form the words, expelling them like a bandage torn from a wound in a swift motion. "My mom died yesterday."

Christy gasped. "I'm so sorry to hear that. What happened?"

Melissa told her the circumstances and funeral arrangements. "Can you come to Decorah for the funeral?"

"Oh, my gosh, Missy, I can't."

Melissa swallowed her disappointment but before she could respond Christy had already jumped ahead.

"I wish I could be there for you, but I'm packing now to go on a cruise with Mom and Katie, just us girls. We do a trip every year without the guys. Katie, you remember Katie, don't you? I can't believe she's fourteen already. Anyway, she has been so excited about it. We are doing a five-day trip to the Caribbean, and it will be the first cruise for her. You know teenage girls…pretty soon she won't want to be with mom and grandma so I'm happy we can do this trip."

Melissa listened with patience before Christy finally stopped and took a breath.

"I understand," Melissa interjected, slipping her comment into a second of silence.

"Mom has insisted she pays for everything. A Caribbean cruise is on her bucket list, and you know she's seventy-five so who knows how much more time we'll have to travel together. I told her no, let's split the cost and we finally worked out that she'd pay for the cruise, and I'd pay for the shore excursions."

While Christy droned on, it occurred to Melissa how much she had envied the family dynamics between Christy and her mother. Their relationship differed in sharp contrast from Melissa's experience. Lydia's passivity manifested with emotional distance and physical absence. Whereas Christy and her mom often joked with each other, even when they disagreed. Her mom's sense of humor had made Melissa laugh too. Whenever Christy participated in a play or cheerleading, her mom would be there, overflowing with praise.

"Oh, gosh Missy, I'm so sorry I can't come, really. I certainly would if I could. I know it must be hard for you since you two were estranged for such a long time. Especially after leaving you so suddenly and never hearing from her again."

Melissa flinched. Christy didn't know about the letters Lydia had sent. Melissa never told anyone about it, not even her father.

"Hey, are you okay?" Christy's voice switched from upbeat to concern. "Have you told your dad about your mom's passing?"

"No." Melissa tightened her jaw.

"You really should call him." Christy's voice lowered to a hush. "Even though he was never very nice to your mom."

"What do you mean?" Melissa asked with surprise.

"I'm sorry, Girlfriend, but didn't you see that? I never told you, but I was always kind of afraid of him. He always seemed, well, a little gruff."

"Really? I guess I thought that's how men are, how marriage worked."

Christy's voice returned to her lighter tone. "Is there anything I can do, Missy?"

Melissa cleared her throat and attempted to hide her dejection. "No, thanks, I'm fine."

"Let's try to get together sometime," Christy said. "You're always invited to our house in Des Moines if you don't mind sharing the space with a spoiled teenager."

Muffled shouts peeled from Christy's phone. "Missy, sorry, I've got to go now, Katie is yelling that she can't find her suitcase, so I have to go help her. I'm so sorry about your mom. Let's talk soon."

"Yes, of course," Melissa said, biting her lip. A sliver of gloom seeped through her, comparing Christy's happy-go-lucky future escapade with her own dismal funeral preparations. Although it was good to hear a familiar voice, she was relieved the conversation ended. Somehow her friend's chipper attitude made her feel worse.

Their conversation brought forth a memory of the high school graduation party and the giggly excitement of planning the festivities. The two girls had worked most of the day decorating. Christy's basement had transformed into a wonderland of balloons in school colors and streamers shimmering in mini disco lights. Hand-made invitations had been distributed to friends at school weeks before with enthusiastic responses. Christy's mom ordered a double-sheet cake from the bakery. Vanilla with double chocolate frosting.

But Melissa never attended the party. Hours before the most important celebration to happen in her young life, she stood trembling with disbelief in the overcast chill of the gray day, barefoot on the chipped concrete driveway of the family home. She could still hear the squeal of the tires careen down the street as she watched her mother drive around the corner and disappear.

***

That evening after dinner of ham sandwiches Gabe sat at the dining room table while Melissa loaded the dishwasher and snapped the appliance door shut. She joined him at the table, sitting adjacent to him. A brochure and business card from Wilson's funeral home lingered at the corner of the tabletop. Gabe leafed through a tabloid-sized local newspaper and stopped at the obituary listings.

"I called my friend, Christy, today and told her about the funeral."

Gabe continued to browse the paper and nodded in silence.

"She can't come."

He looked up at her. "I've made a couple calls, too. The

obit will probably be in the paper tomorrow. Word around here spreads fast." He returned his attention to the paper.

Melissa drummed her fingers in a slow rhythm on the table. The sun had set, and night settled in. A soft glow from the dining room light cast shadows in the darkened corners of the room. She squirmed in her chair, hesitating to broach an unpleasant topic but curiosity prodded her.

"Talking with Christy today made me think about..." She took a deep inhale. "About the past."

Gabe folded the newspaper and pushed it away from him. He turned his attention toward her.

"Your letter you sent me about coming here — you said you knew about the history between me and Mom." Melissa pressed her palms onto the dining room table. "What did she tell you about the day she left me?"

"Oh, yes." He folded his hands on the table. "Well, what do you want to know?"

His offer loomed too broad to answer. Surely, he knew about the events surrounding that day. Probably much more about her childhood than she assumed. Stories told by her mother. He was practically a stranger to her. What did he really understand about her and what had happened so long ago? She tightened her lips together, sorting out where to begin.

His tone lowered to almost a whisper. "I know it was a tough time for everyone then. Lydia had tremendous guilt about the way she left. She wanted to wait until you were away at college so it might prepare you better."

Melissa frowned. "How can you ever prepare for your parent's breakup?"

She gazed out the window into the darkness, gathering her thoughts. Would he judge her side of the story? She wanted him to know, to purge herself of the pain of it.

"It's okay to talk to me," he said.

She nodded and drew a breath. "I knew there were things that weren't right in my family. But I didn't know how bad it was until the fight they had that day."

Gabe frowned. "Lydia told me there had been an argument with Robert."

Melissa's head buzzed. The argument. The scene played out in her mind. Its haunting persistence played in a disjointed sequence. Twisted faces, bulging eyes. Her father clenching his fists, tensing his arms, holding a pose as if ready to strike.

"What do you remember about it?" Gabe asked.

Was it her mom's trembling that vibrated against Melissa's chest or her own shaking? Her head buried into her mother's embrace, tears soaking the cotton shirt that smelled of lavender mingled with fresh sweat. "Please don't go." Fractured words uttered between quivering sobs.

Melissa tightened her jaw. "I don't remember the context of the fight, what they said, even though I've tried. It all seemed incomprehensible. Accusations spewing out like venom. It was the first and only time I had seen my dad like that."

Gabe waited as Melissa wiped away tears.

"I remember Mom grabbed my hand and pulled me outside to the driveway. I thought she'd take me wherever she was going, but then I saw her suitcase next to the car. I knew she meant to leave…alone."

"Did she say anything to you?" Gabe asked.

"She said something like everything would be okay. I couldn't think straight. It all seemed like a bad dream. I didn't ask her where she was going or why I couldn't go with her. Christ, I was just seventeen, and yeah, pretty much led a sheltered life. She promised to contact me. But I never heard from her."

Gabe didn't look surprised by her tale, but his expression remained sympathetic. "She never intended it to come to that. She hadn't planned on what happened. The situation was … complicated."

Melissa turned away from him and rested her forehead in

her hand.

"Dad closed in behind us yelling something about not getting a dime from him. That's when she threw her suitcase in the trunk and jumped into the car. I remember the look she gave me. A mix of terror and sadness. The car window was closed, and she mouthed the words, I love you. Then she just drove away."

Melissa swiped clenched knuckles across her mouth to steady her quivering lips.

"I'm glad you told me," Gabe said. He reached over and put his hand on hers. Neither one said anything for the next few minutes.

"Hey," Gabe said, pulling his palm off her hand and lifting her chin. "I have something I want to show you."

Melissa wiped her cheek with the back of her hand. "What is it?" She rose from the chair and followed him up the stairs to the locked door at the end of the hall.

Chapter 10

Tuesday Evening

Gabe led Melissa to the closed door at the end of the upstairs hallway.

"That door is locked," she said. "I heard a phone ringing from up here when you were gone this morning and when I got here, the ringing stopped. I turned the doorknob, and it didn't budge."

Gabe looked amused. "You're right," he said, twisting the stationary brass knob. "It doesn't move."

"So, why is the room locked?"

"Who says it's locked?" He pushed the door open.

Melissa raised her eyebrows. "I swear…"

He interrupted her. "These old houses have their quirks. The door doesn't latch right, but it opens and closes easily enough. I just haven't gotten around to fixing it." He entered the darkened room and switched on an overhead light. She trailed behind.

The scent of oil paint and turpentine evoked a memory of watching her mother brush blobs of color on canvas. An empty easel stood in one corner of the room. A crumpled, paint-spotted rag draped across the top.

Melissa held a sense of being a visitor in someone else's sanctuary.

"Are all these pieces her artwork?"

"Yes," Gabe said. "This is her studio."

Pastel-colored papers lay in a neat stack on a rectangular table on the other side of the room. Colored pencils peppered the surface in a rainbow array. She lingered by the sketch pad sprawled across its tabletop to study a charcoal drawing. Bold strokes of black charcoal and highlights of white chalk created depth and contrast on the gray paper. A solitary woman stood on a high cliff with her back to the observer, facing a deep canyon. Long, dark hair swept backward in tendrils, blown by a gentle wind.

Gabe moved next to her and looked at the drawing. "She called this one Dust and Wind. One time I asked her why she named it that.

He hesitated, looking upward as if to capture her words from the air. "We are all part of nature – physical nature, human nature – at the mercy of its fury as well as its incredible beauty. It's constant, yet always changes."

"That's beautiful," Melissa said. "The sentiment surprises me. I don't recall Mom being so philosophical."

"Ah, there's her phone," Gabe said pointing to the office desk and chair near the doorway. "That's probably what you heard ringing this morning." He picked up the device, cradling it for a moment as if it were a talisman. A faraway sadness reflected in his eyes. He set it down with a sigh and leaned against the desk.

"She loved this studio. It was a special place for her." He shook his head. "I can't believe she's gone. I halfway expect her to come in at any moment and sit down, ready to paint." He dropped into the chair with a weary exhale.

Melissa picked up the drawing on the table. "I remember Mom would play music while she painted. She'd sit at her drawing board as I twirled in circles until I was dizzy. Then we'd dance together like ballerinas." Melissa turned toward Gabe. "I never saw her dance after I got older. She became more withdrawn and preoccupied."

"I wish I would have known you then." Gabe looked at her with downturned lips. For a brief moment, she questioned why he said this but brushed it aside. Perhaps his comment posed a regret of the absence of children in his life.

Melissa meandered around the room browsing the images. Photos and drawings hung on the wall, taped up in a haphazard jumble.

"Her drawing board was set up in the basement of our house," Melissa said. "As a kid, I would sit at my little desk beside her and play with the coloring books she gave me." A fleeting smile crossed her face. "She always praised my crayon scribbles, then hung them on the wall by her drawing board."

Gabe nodded, "Lydia told me about that, she referred to the room as her…how did she say it?" They both spoke the words simultaneously. "Dungeon retreat."

"My dad never liked it when she busied herself with her art. He would slam doors, pace around, or demand her attention whenever she spent time downstairs. He thought it was a foolish pastime. He'd criticize her about what she should be doing instead."

Melissa's face pinched with mock irritation. "My God, Lydia," she mimicked her father's deeper voice. "This place looks like a pigsty. You need to keep this house clean instead of playing all day." Melissa crossed her arms and frowned. "Dad was adamant about order and cleanliness. Mom insisted I keep my toys in my room and not have them in other parts of the house, especially when he got home from work."

"It sounds like Robert got angry a lot."

"I guess I see that now as an adult." She stretched her arms toward a side table by the window, reaching her fingers to feel the pad of paper there. A pencil rolled toward the indention created by her touch and came to rest against her hand. She lingered there for a moment and then drew back, her arms circling herself in a hug.

"Back then I thought she must have done something wrong to make Dad yell at her. I just didn't know what that was." Melissa turned to Gabe. "Maybe I was just relieved his disapproval wasn't directed at me."

She pivoted toward the window. A framed drawing piqued her interest. Approaching it for a closer look, she eased it from its perch and held it with both hands. The portrait of a young woman with black hair and blue eyes stared at her, like she had just looked into a mirror from the past. "Oh, my God, Gabe, that's me." The skillful artistry captured a praiseworthy accuracy.

He nodded. "She drew that using a photo from your high school days. Your mom thought about you a lot, Melissa, more than you know. I think she drew that picture to feel closer to you."

He rose from the chair and stood next to her. "She never stopped thinking about you, how you were doing, and what your life was like."

Melissa studied the portrait with cool reserve. The rendition presented a moment in time when youth and innocence existed. A time when they were a family. Yet the subtle coloring hinted at a feeling short of joyful. A static moment brought forth and assembled from depths of memory, clinging to something out of reach.

"We had so many plans for the future," Gabe said. "Maybe sell the farm, retire someplace warm. That probably would have been in the next few years. Sixty-five is just around the corner for me."

He looked at her. "We talked about going to San Francisco. Visit the art museums. Try to find you."

Melissa spun around. "To find me?"

He nodded. "We had an address, but no way of knowing if you still lived there. I tried to convince her we should go and just take a chance. But I think she feared rejection. To feel that pain. We put off the decision, pushing it back to sometime soon— or maybe next year." He shoved his hands in his pockets and looked away from her.

Melissa eased the drawing back on its wall hanger. The thought of her mom's unannounced appearance in San Francisco spurred a question of how she would have reacted. Nothing could change the past, and she doubted anything could change her mind about her mother, despite these childhood memories.

Chapter 11

Tuesday Evening

Gabe sat at the desk in the studio and rifled through the side drawer.

Melissa watched him. "What are you doing?" she asked.

"There's something else you need to see," he said. A moment later he muttered. "Here they are." He pulled out a couple of envelopes and held them in her direction. "Lydia kept these for years. I know she hoped someday you would read them. I think maybe this would be a good time to do that. It may help you understand."

"What are they?" She stepped closer, grasping the pastel-colored stationery.

"Letters she wrote to you. She wanted to connect, to tell you things you needed to know. But these were returned unopened."

She rubbed the envelopes between her thumb and fingers. The paper felt velvety and smooth, like the fabric of a well-worn garment. Her mother's cursive handwriting flowed across the address line. Scratched across the face of the envelope Melissa recognized her own scrawled response. Return to Sender. Anger toward her mother had directed the response. The action made more of a statement than any reply she could have written.

"Yes, I remember getting these letters. I never imagined I would see them again." She gripped the thin parcel and sank into a chair next to him.

He leaned toward her. "Why did you send them back? Weren't you curious about what she had to say?"

She clenched her teeth. "I convinced myself whatever news it brought could only be my mother wanting something from me. Something I wasn't ready to give." Her face tensed with the memory. "I was so mad at her. That overshadowed any curiosity. I didn't want to deal with any emotional conflicts or family complications."

Melissa pointed her scowl in his direction. "You need to understand, Gabe. It had been years without hearing from her. She was absent for anything meaningful to me — high school graduation, birthdays, even when I got my associate degree. Dad told me he invited her to the commencement, but she never replied. That was it for me. I was done hoping things would change and vowed to live without her — without a mother."

She placed the letters on the table, pressing her fingertips against them for a moment, then drew back.

Gabe's face tightened like he had just tasted something sour. He leaned his elbows on the table and picked up the envelopes, adjusting his eyeglasses to examine them.

"I think she sent this when you must have been around 21 or so, judging from the postmark. Probably working on your bachelor's degree by then."

Melissa crossed her arms against her chest.

"Hmm, this one is postmarked 2005, the year she and I were married." His eyes rested on the letters and back to Melissa. "I know she had written more but never mailed them. After getting the last letter returned, she never sent another one. I wanted her to try again but she didn't want to even talk about it. I think she accepted it as her failure that she had to live with." He squinted at Melissa. "Maybe she felt somehow she deserved it, but I think all she wanted was to reconcile."

A surge of indignation boiled up within her. "Where was mom

when I needed her?" Her tone sharpened and she felt the heat in her cheeks. "Maybe she was ready to reconcile, but I wasn't." Melissa faced him for a moment and shook her head. Her fists clenched in her lap. "I had come to terms with my life without her."

The bitterness of her words, so long festering in her head, fell out jagged and cutting. "My decision to return the letters empowered me to believe that I was sending my message — you can't hurt me anymore. It was my turn to abandon her — to make her feel the pain that I contended with."

Gabe's expression softened and he leaned forward with elbows on his knees, fingers interlaced.

"Melissa, I wasn't there when you were growing up, so I don't know how things were in your family. But I know there are always two sides to a story. So, I can only give you my perspective from what I know from my own experience. And what Lydia told me."

Melissa closed her eyes and rubbed her fingers across her forehead.

He pressed closer to her pinched face. "I understand you've lived with this pain for a long time thinking she didn't care about you. But that wasn't the case. She tried to find you. Robert refused to cooperate or let her know where you were."

Melissa shrank back, shaking her head in disbelief. "Dad wouldn't have done that. He told me he never heard from her."

Gabe shrugged. "You were almost 18 when she left. Weeks away from legally becoming an adult. Robert wasn't obligated to provide any information about you. He withheld the information because he wanted to punish Lydia."

"Even if that were true, which I disagree, she could have found other ways to find me. Like…social media?"

"Remember, this was the time before many people had cell phones and technology wasn't like it is now."

"Why didn't she get a private detective?"

"It was a tough time for her, without financial resources or means. She had to get her own life in order first."

Melissa frowned. "So how did she get my address?"

"From your Aunt Irene."

"What? Really? I barely heard from her or my uncle. I think they disapproved of the divorce and Dad's second marriage. Dad had never been very close with his brother, anyway."

Gabe nodded. "Well, your mom didn't know how Irene found out about Robert not sharing where you were. But Irene must have discovered the situation and felt some sympathy.

"Why do you say that?"

"Lydia told me that years after the divorce your aunt had called her. That's when Lydia got your address in San Francisco. I guess Irene didn't think it was right for a mother to not know her own daughter's whereabouts."

The new revelations shook Melissa. Her mother chose to leave, to forget the family. Melissa witnessed that firsthand. Her mom's absence fit the scenario her dad had laid out. He wouldn't have lied just to keep them apart. Would he? Aunt Irene had never mentioned a word about the part Gabe claimed she played.

Gabe gathered the letters together. "It's okay if you don't want these. I understand." He dropped them into the trash can with one toss.

Melissa looked at him. "But...don't you want them?"

He leaned back in the chair. "They're not for me. They were meant for you." His gaze turned toward the window.

Melissa stared at the unopened envelopes in the trash can. These were the same rejected letters that once passed through her own hands. Now they stubbornly demanded her attention, archived until this very moment. She sighed. For the first time, curiosity begged her to tear into words that had been sealed for nearly two decades.

"Oh, for heaven's sake, Gabe." Her expression changed to a pout, and she retrieved the letters.

Chapter 12

Tuesday Evening

May 1999
Dear Melissa,
I am writing to you in the month that you turn 21 years old. I'm not sure if this letter will reach you, but I had to try.
You are now legally an adult in every sense. I imagine you are in college now. That's what Robert and I always wanted for you. I just hope you are happy and healthy, wherever you are, whatever you're doing. I want so much to talk to you, to hear your voice, to hug you. I daydream about when you were a child, the two of us together, laughing, reading, playing. Just sharing time. Watching you grow up. I think I was a good mother then.
But things changed. When I left on that day, I felt incapable of being a good parent. Your dad told me I was lousy at motherhood, lacking to teach you discipline and obedience. I failed you in many more ways, I suppose, missing your 18th birthday and graduations. Probably many other times when I should have been there. I'm so sorry for that and the pain it must have caused you.
You may wonder why I left on that day after

the huge argument between me and Robert. It was more like an escape. I had thought about walking out when you were younger but couldn't do it. I felt it was important that you had a home with both parents. When your grandma died, you were only 12. I thought about how she struggled to raise me alone. We had so many hardships. I didn't want either of us to be in that situation.

Most likely you witnessed the friction between your dad and me even though no one talked about it. Although we bickered a lot, I thought Robert was a good father to you. I would never have left you with him if I thought he would hurt you in any way.

The trouble was between him and me. It took years of living with him for my sense of identity to drip away. The constant belittlement and gaslighting were very subtle. There came a point where I felt invisible, like I was nothing. Couple's counseling may have helped, but he refused. He told me I was too sensitive and overly emotional, telling me whatever problems we had could be solved between us. I trusted he was right, but nothing changed, it only got worse.

The day I left I didn't know what to do. I had no job, no income, just my car, and a suitcase. If it weren't for Angela, my only friend, I don't know what I would have done.

Angela and I worked together at the Art Alliance. She took me into her home when I had no place to go. Although she is just 10 years older than you, I have learned many things from her about confidence and gratefulness. Recognizing emotional abuse and low self-esteem has helped me discover who I am. It has taken me a long time to find my way out of the darkness. Angela and I are happy living together. Her influence helped me get a job as an assistant in a small art studio. I'm considering taking a few evening college classes too, maybe even getting a degree.

Memories of us together are precious to me. When you were little your favorite book was about fairies and magic. One day you asked me if magic was real, and I told you many things in the world are unexplained. We think what we see and feel is the way things are. But maybe we can be a little more like fairies and find the magic that is all around us.

I hope you will be able to see the magical things in the world. Perhaps it will be a random acquaintance who will change your life or a coincidence that challenges your assumptions. Be open to meaningful connections that may come from unlikely or surprising places.

I love you,
Mom

***

Melissa placed the letter on the table after she read it to Gabe. Words contrived by a woman desperate to justify her actions weren't surprising.

"Well, I suppose that's intended to be an apology," Melissa said. "But I remember it a little differently."

"How so?" Gabe asked, leaning forward in his chair.

"When she left, the weight of the world dumped on me. Maybe the problem was between my parents, but I felt at fault. Somehow never quite living up to her expectations. Like I should have somehow been better at making her happy and couldn't. But she was the adult. She was supposed to fix things, not me. Instead, she chose to run away."

Gabe shook his head. "You know now it wasn't because of you, right?"

Melissa shrugged. Rising from her chair, she stepped to the window and gazed at the risen moon peeking above the horizon.

"Mom never confronted Dad about anything. He'd come home late from work without much explanation. He'd put her down a lot. Demean her. It was like she was a child, cowering from him. When she lost her job, she retreated into her own world. After school, I'd find her in her bathrobe, watching soap operas. Most of the time, I did all the cleaning and cooking. She lacked interest in anything, including me. Looking back, I wanted her to be stronger. I just wanted everyone to be happy. At the same time, I accepted that's the way it was because I didn't know how to change it."

She crossed her arms. "I think Mom coped by believing in magic and illusion." Melissa stretched the word magic for emphasis. "She stopped painting, but I would find doodles on scratchpads of fairies, or bizarre animals with wings floating in cartoon landscapes. Fantasy stuff like that."

The vividness of the dream flashed in her mind along with its emotional potency. She rubbed her temples as if to squeeze out the intrusion.

Gabe nodded. "Depression about her marriage probably overwhelmed her. Robert treated her differently than he did you. At least, that's what she told me," Gabe said.

"Mom may have thought Dad was a good father, and she was right that he never physically hurt me, but I was left to cope with the fallout after the divorce."

"What did he tell you about what happened after she left?"

"Not much. I only knew she lived with another woman somewhere. If I asked too many questions, he would either get angry or withdrawn. I preferred silence over those choices, so I avoided the topic."

Melissa pivoted toward Gabe. "You know, Dad never mentioned the woman's name. He just referred to her as your mother's girlfriend. The call you got this morning was the same Angela she mentioned in the letter, wasn't it?"

Gabe nodded. "Yes, I called her earlier and left a message about —" His voice lowered to a hushed tone— "about your mom's passing. I thought she would want to know."

"Maybe Mom's lack of friends was because she was so timid," Melissa said.

"Or maybe because she didn't want to upset Robert." A hint of defensiveness charged his voice.

"What do you mean?"

"Lydia told me he'd get mad if she wanted to go out with a friend or invite someone over. He told her that because she was married, she needed to focus on family life."

Melissa scratched her head. "Whatever the reason, I don't recall any friendships she had. I never met Angela."

Gabe raised his eyebrows. "Hmm, Lydia told me she had known Angela for quite a while. You were just a freshman in high school when they met at work. Two years before she left."

Melissa returned to the chair and sat next to Gabe. "So, what you're saying is Mom hid her friendship with this Angela person for some reason, maybe because it would upset Dad. Right?"

Gabe shrugged. "All I know is what she told me."

Exhaustion from the conversation left her muddled, like any energy she once had drained into a quagmire of confusion. She excused herself to her room for the evening. Thoughts about the letter, Angela, and her dad felt like puzzle pieces forced into a previously completed frame.

Why did her mom feel the need to hide a friendship? What's the big deal? Did her father forbid her to have friends?

Lying in bed that evening, fragmented recollections bounced

around behind her closed eyes. Once, she came home early from school. An unfamiliar car had been parked in the driveway. Inside, her mom and a woman, younger than her mother, chatted at the dining room table. Her mom acted odd when she saw Melissa, springing from the chair in a nervous huff.

The stranger's slim frame lacked feminine curves, or maybe just minimized underneath the loose-fitting polo shirt and baggy jeans. If it weren't for her oval face and creamy skin, she could have been mistaken for a boy at a distance. Her mother introduced her companion as someone from work. The name, as well as details of the conversion, escaped Melissa's memory. But she did recall being struck by her forthright way of speaking. Direct and confident. Unlike her mother.

Melissa never saw the woman again. The unexpected memory provided another example of being pushed away and kept in the dark about something as innocent as a friendship. The thought reaffirmed her belief about the deception that came so easily for her mother.

Just before drifting off to sleep, a sudden urge to call her father nagged her. But it could wait until the morning.

Chapter 13

Wednesday Morning

Hammering outside Melissa's bedroom window had awakened her that morning. Gabe must have risen early to continue work on the doghouse. She sipped her morning coffee and watched him from the kitchen window. Doc lay by her chair, his eyes focused on the outside activity.

She reached down and stroked Doc's furry head. "Next, he'll fix the roof. Your house will be as good as new."

The dog's tail thumped a slow beat on the floor.

Sauntering into the living room, she set the coffee cup beside her phone on the side table. It had been several months since she had talked to her dad, partly due to the time difference from San Francisco and Italy. She seldom enjoyed their conversations. Most of the mundane chitchat revolved around himself or his third wife, Francesca. But he had a right to know about her mom. Whether he cared or not was another matter. She punched in the numbers. Might as well get it over with.

"Hi Dad. How are you? What time is it there in Italy?"

Well, hello!" His voice sounded upbeat. "It's past 3:00 in the afternoon, so it's time for wine." He laughed. "I'm at the cafe waiting for Francesca to get here. What's new?"

Melissa tightened her grip on the phone. "I have some bad news. I'm in Iowa."

"What? Did you say Iowa? That is bad news." He laughed at

his own joke. Melissa tightened her lips into a thin line, waiting to regain his attention.

"What the hell are you doing there?" he asked.

"Well, I was going to call you after I got home, but decided you should know something now."

"Sounds serious. You getting married?"

"No, Dad." She rolled her eyes. Taking a deep breath, she paced the floor, stopping next to the photo of her mom and Gabe. "Well, you should know Mom died on Monday."

"Oh, what from?" he asked.

"Aneurysm."

He fell silent for several seconds, then spoke a phrase in Italian, his voice muffled like he held the phone away from him. She picked up the word vino. Tapping her foot, she waited for his response.

"Sorry, the waiter came by. So how did you find out?" His casual tone sounded as if she had just informed him about the weather.

"I got a letter from Gabe."

"Who?"

"Her husband, Gabe."

"Oh, the guy that was her high school boyfriend? Huh, that's a surprise."

"Why? That she remarried? You've been married twice since her."

"That's different. At least I know which team I'm on."

"What are you talking about?" she said, impatient with his flippant attitude. Her father liked bending the discussions to what he wanted to talk about.

"You never knew, did you?"

"Knew what? You're not making sense."

"Did you know about Angela?"

His question surprised her with the turn of the topic. How did he know Angela?

"Yes, her friend," she said.

He snorted. "Friend? Jesus, Melissa. Angela was your mom's girlfriend. A goddamn lesbian. She's the reason your mom left us. Your mom went away to live a gay life. We'd still be a family if it wasn't for the damn queer bitch. She turned your mom into a lesbo."

Melissa's hand trembled. She fell into a chair and clenched the cushion to steady herself.

"You still there? Melissa?" Without waiting for a response, he rambled on.

"How could a responsible mother leave her husband and child to go live a twisted life like that? Well, she did. She left us, Melissa. Didn't care about us and only thought about herself."

Cupping her forehead in her hand, she inhaled a quick breath as if she'd just been punched in the gut. "I didn't know. Why didn't you ever tell me?"

"Shit, what man wants to announce his wife left him for another woman? I don't blame you for shutting her out all these years. I'm surprised you're there now. What's the point? It's too late for her to beg sympathy. People yammer on about forgiveness, but she didn't deserve any from either one of us. All that talk about forgiveness and letting things go. It's bullshit."

"I just can't believe it," Melissa shook her head. "All this time I thought it was my fault."

"Hell, no. it wasn't you, it wasn't me," he snarled. "Your mom was weak, easily persuaded to believe all kinds of goddamn shit. Not like us. You and I are alike. Tough and rational. We don't let anyone push us around."

At that moment, Melissa didn't feel tough or rational. Confused and hurt, yes. Did her father believe his own story? Although he had his faults, she always trusted him to tell her the truth. His strong will shielded her in difficult times, helping her through college and negotiating for the apartment in the city. He had been, after all, the parent that stayed.

"Look, I'm sorry you lost your mom, but she got what she asked for after she left us. Nobody would blame you for being angry and avoiding her all these years. It's righteous anger."

She debated whether to tell him about the letters but bit her lip. She didn't want to fuel his fire.

You okay, sweetheart?" he said, slipping into a calm voice.

She exhaled a whimpering breath. "Yeah, I'm fine, Dad."

Melissa narrowed her eyes at her mother's smiling portrait.

"Hey, at least I hope you get some of the money back that she took from me in the divorce."

His brusque comment made her flinch. "Dad, why would she leave me anything? I'm not expecting any of her money. Besides, it's not like she probably had much. There's nothing extravagant about their lifestyle here, believe me."

"Okay, sweetie, I have to go, Francesca just arrived. I'm glad you called. Take care of yourself. Talk to you later."

Gabe came inside the house a few minutes after Melissa ended the phone call. She sat at the kitchen table finishing her coffee as he washed his hands in the sink.

"What's up with you? You look kind of glum," he said.

She faced him without smiling. "I just talked to my dad."

"Oh?" He poured a cup of the brew and settled into the chair across from her at the table. He took a sip.

Melissa shifted in her chair. She traced her finger around the rim of her empty cup. Doc lapped water from his bowl.

"So?" Gabe said.

"Well, he told me something about Mom I didn't know."

He leaned forward and rested his arms on the table. "What?"

"It was about Angela and Mom. How close were they?"

His eyes cast downward at his fingers tapping a slow rhythm on the side of the cup he held. "I never asked Lydia about the details of their life together. Or judged her. I only know they were very close."

"Was Angela really her lesbian lover?" Melissa blurted out

the words like bitter fruit.

Gabe's cheeks flushed a pale pink, but he didn't seem surprised. "Angela changed Lydia. Brought her out of her shell. Encouraged her talent. They were inseparable for the three years they lived together."

Melissa tried to imagine this part of her mother she knew nothing about. "What happened? Why only three years?"

"I'm not sure. What I do know is that life isn't always black or white. Relationships between two people can be very different from what it may appear to someone else. Love is love. When you feel it, you can't deny it, even when disapproved of by others."

Melissa tilted her head. "You're quite a philosopher."

"Not really. I just have a lot of life experience, I guess. I'm old." He grinned.

Melissa sighed. "That type of love has not happened to me. The over-the-moon experience that changes you, I mean."

"Even when you were married?"

"Maybe I felt that a little bit at first. But most of my relationships have been, well, disappointing. I guess you might say I'm very selective." A pleasant image of Jeremy's smile flashed into her thoughts. The text yesterday he sent asking her out perhaps needed a reply.

"Did your dad say anything else?" Gabe asked.

She emerged from her thought about Jeremy and shook her head. "Nothing important."

Gabe turned solemn. "I wonder if you can help me with a task?"

"What is it? I'm not very good at fixing doghouses."

His lips turned up for a moment. "No, I've got that covered. It's something I'm having a hard time with, and I'd like to get your take on it."

Melissa saw the pain in his face. "Of course, whatever I can do to help."

He nodded. It's better if I just show you." He motioned his head toward the stairway. She followed him upstairs.

Chapter 14

Wednesday Morning

Gabe led her to the master suite upstairs. He entered the large room while Melissa stood at the doorway. Her eyes widened, taking in the scene before her.

Dresses and sweaters lay in disarray across the bed. Multi-colored blouses were piled on top of each other on the upholstered wing chair in the corner. The closet door gaped opened, revealing a rack of women's clothing squeezed together in the narrow space. Their alignment created a rainbow effect. Melissa recognized this organizing habit her mother favored.

Gabe swept a hand around the spacious room. His eyes moistened. "I have to find a burial dress. The funeral home needs it today."

He plopped down on the edge of the bed, sinking in a chaotic sea of textures and fabrics. His head slumped between hunched shoulders.

"I've always been good at problem solving, but this has me stumped. You'd think it'd be easy to just pick something, but ... well, it's not." He shrugged and looked toward the closet.

"And you've been trying to find something that will be just right," Melissa said in a sympathetic voice, scanning the jumble.

Gabe nodded. "I know this may sound silly, but every time I pick a dress or sweater, it reminds me of the last time she wore it, what we were doing. I can picture her smiling at me. Whenever we dressed up to go out, we'd joke about how we clean up pretty damn good." His voice cracked as he touched his wedding ring. "I just can't get beyond that to decide what to choose."

Melissa walked over to him and rested her hand on his shoulder. "Maybe I can help." She turned toward the closet. "Let's see what we can find." Her nose wrinkled as the scent of stale perfume escaped when she slid the clothes along the closet rack.

She sifted through casual blouses, a few blazers, flannel shirts, jeans, and dress pants. Old t-shirts with various printed designs and goofy memes lay folded on an open shelf. A pink t-shirt read Housework can't kill you but why take the chance? She flipped through the quirky attire as if perusing greeting cards on a store display. A black long-sleeved shirt with white letters read Live, Life, Love. A threadbare, dingy t-shirt with a faded cartoon of a cow read 1977 Iowa State Fair. She plunged deeper into the hunt, finding a plain, black dress, a few dark-colored skirts, plaid, and paisley work shirts.

A light blue dress caught her eye, the material unlike the others. She grasped the hanger and removed it from the recess of the closet to view in brighter light. Lace ran lengthwise along the long sleeves and across the scooped neckline. A modest sprinkle of rhinestones adorned the shoulders and trickled down the front in a sparkling cascade. The sleek bodice cinched at the waist. Shimmering satin extended to just below knee length.

Gabe stared at the dress. His chin inched up. "That was her wedding dress."

Melissa touched the luxurious fabric, indulging in the sensation of delicate lace and satin under her fingertips. Her mother had always been a slim, size eight. She pulled the dress against her body, smoothing the fabric with her palm. For a fleeting moment she imagined the fragrance of roses and something like a spark, a pulse of energy filled with joyfulness transcended from another time.

Holding the dress outward in Gabe's direction, she looked at

him without saying a word, only a subtle smile.
"I think she'd like that one," he said.

***

Gabe left to deliver the dress to the funeral home while Melissa and Doc stayed at the house. She begged off the invitation to accompany him and instead offered to tidy up the clothing blizzard.

Tackling the chore of storing her mother's clothes into boxes flowed with a detached efficiency at first. Sorting, folding, stacking, and packing streamed in a mechanical rhythm. These items were simply a collection of garments to discard. No longer troubled with.

The rapidity of her pace slowed when she recognized a blouse with a colorful floral pattern. Her mom had bought it on one of their shopping trips together. Melissa stopped and reached for it, bringing it to her nose. The scent so familiar it evoked a sudden memory. A sensation of arms wrapped around her within a landscape of flowers, ear pressed against a beating heart. Comfort and tenderness in the embrace. She breathed in again before relinquishing the blouse into the box of clothes.

The two of them often shopped together at the mall, up until the time Melissa could drive the family car and go alone or with Christy. Melissa's clothing tastes leaned toward simplicity — black turtlenecks, unadorned fabrics. Her mother preferred ruffles and frills. Prom shopping her junior year provoked disagreement when Lydia raved about the dress with a hideous, high-laced neckline. Melissa had insisted on the flattering sweetheart style with spaghetti straps – the one finally agreed upon by both. Despite their differences in style, Melissa smiled with the pleasant memory of happier times.

She shuttered the closet. Her packing task finished, she eased her way to the bedroom door and lingered there. With Gabe gone, the house felt hushed. Sunshine radiated through the high clerestory windows, warming the second story hallway running between the master bedroom and studio. Daylight and shadows filtered through tree leaves danced upon the floor and wall like a monotone kaleidoscope. A glow shimmered across the door at the end of the hall. The mesmerizing pattern of movement drew her in as she approached the studio. She pushed the door open.

Her eyes darted around the room. Two letters rested on the desk. She had attended to one, but the other had been left unread from last night. Sitting at the desk, she picked up the unopened envelope and studied it before tearing open the flap and removing the stationery.

Chapter 15

Second Letter to Melissa

August 2005
Dear Melissa,
I know you returned my first letter unopened, and I understand if you are still angry or disappointed in me. Maybe your heart has softened because you are reading this now.
I've met a wonderful man. His name is Gabe Murphy. We went to high school together and dated before I met Robert. We reconnected at our high school reunion last June in Des Moines. He is a widower and lives on his dairy farm in northeast Iowa near Decorah.
My big news is we are getting married in September! I've enclosed the wedding invitation that I designed. I never thought at 50 years old I'd be getting married again after being single these past 13 years... or living on a farm for that matter! I'm taking his last name, so I'll be Lydia Murphy.
My wedding dress is so beautiful, I wish you could see it. The blue reminds me of the color of your eyes. Remember how we used to shop together when we wanted something special? I think we'd both agree this dress is perfect.

There is something very important for you to know that we need to talk about in person. I don't want to put it in a letter. Please come to the wedding. It will be small and informal. I want you to meet Gabe. You'll like him. He's a very good and honorable man.

Please come or call me. Oh, I just got this new flip phone thingy too that I can carry around with me. Technology seems to be getting ahead of me! My new contact information is below.

Love you,
Mom

Melissa finished reading and returned the letter beside the first one on the desk. She leaned back in the chair and closed her eyes. Would she had agreed to attend a wedding when she was 27 years old? Such an event would have not held much joy for her. Raw bitterness permeated everything related to her mother then. She would have scorned the invite. This unread letter had been sent back unopened, just like the previous one. Yet now she wondered what path her life may have taken if she made a different choice.

She imagined her mother picking out the wedding dress for the happy occasion. The same dress Melissa and Gabe had just selected for her funeral. A shiver ran through her. So strange the letter mentioned the dress. *I wish you could see it,* the words her mom used so many years ago penned on paper.

The most baffling content piqued her curiosity. What did her mother mean about something that needed spoken in person? Something unsuited to describe in a letter. Perhaps an explanation about Angela? Did she love another woman? More likely, some kind of shocking dirt on her dad. Crap her mother thought would sour Melissa toward him. Maybe even create a rift between them.

The divorce had been very acrimonious. On the other hand, she didn't picture her mother possessing a mean streak. Timid and misguided, yes, but her faults didn't include vindictiveness.

Her dad had been such a wreck after Lydia left. The rumors around the upscale neighborhood probably didn't help. According to Christy's mom, there had been talk whispered about Robert's quick remarriage a few months after the divorce. Gossip insinuated the breakup had been caused by an extramarital affair between her dad and Heather Miner, a divorcee he met at his fitness club. Melissa didn't know much about her stepmother and didn't care. She had dismissed the neighbor's prattle as wagging tongues of old ladies with nothing better to do. The remarriage did happen fast, though. By the time they wed one weekend at a Las Vegas chapel, Melissa lived in a college dorm a thousand plus miles away from Iowa. Contact with her new stepmother ranged from seldom to none and consisted of brief holidays or school breaks. Melissa held a neutral regard toward her, but then again, the woman must have made her dad happy for a while. Until their divorce, anyway.

What other secrets did she not know? A gnawing feeling prickled her about Gabe. She liked him, but felt he held back something. Whatever the intention of her mother's message, speculation proved useless now.

The chime of the doorbell interrupted her thoughts.

Chapter 16

Lydia and Gabe 1977

The weather at the Iowa State Fair engulfed the fairgrounds like every year – hot and steamy. Late summer air drifted aromas of fried foods, caramel apples, and popcorn, all blended in a fragrant stew of sweet and savory. Thousands of visitors throughout the Midwest roamed the acres of ground; farmers, city dwellers, and everyone in between, for its ten days of entertainment. Myriad forms of thrills enticed young and old to the festive atmosphere of carnival, games, exhibits, and farm animals.

Heat and humidity did not deter Lydia from attending her favorite annual event. She loved the excitement of the fair. Living in the capital city of Des Moines all her 22 years, the State Fair offered a chance to learn about the state. The wide range of animals fascinated her. She relished the opportunity to get an up-close look at livestock brought in by farmers to parade around arenas. Large barns erected to house the animals carried the scent of hay and unaccustomed, but pleasant smells. The language of chickens, pigs, horses, cows, and sheep produced a cacophony of vocalizations. Fuzzy chicks, wriggling piglets, long-legged foals, big-eyed calves, and sweet lambs mesmerized her. To Lydia, this was as exotic to her as any circus menagerie.

In addition to these creatures, handicrafts, textiles, agricultural produce, and garden flora were displayed in permanent buildings. The Cultural building, a 3-story brick structure that housed sculpture, crafts, and fine art became a favorite attraction. She absorbed the atmosphere of the creative collections. Her sense of expansive worlds blossomed, breathing in not only the artistic possibility but imagination of what kind of lives the artists led.

For the past year, her role as Administrative Assistant at the Iowa Art Council was to help the organization's directors with scheduling, filing, and general duties. When her boss asked her to volunteer to work as an official greeter at the building's entrance, she jumped at the chance. Her duties included helping visitors with questions, distributing maps of the fairgrounds, or pointing out directions to exhibits. She enjoyed chatting with people, even though Robert had often disapproved of her engaging in conversations, especially with men. He frequently chastised her for flirting or being too talkative. But here out of his earshot, she allowed her natural inclinations to flow with the carefree nature of the fair.

Instead of going straight home after finishing work on the first day, she indulged in a stroll around the bustling fairgrounds. A sign promising views of newborn calves inside the nearby cattle barn beckoned her into the barn. She checked her watch. Robert worked out of town that week. He expected her to come directly home after work and called every evening at 7:00. But certainly a few hours spent between work and home wouldn't hurt anything. Moments spent without explanation to anyone, especially Robert, seemed a precious luxury. She had time before his call.

Engrossed in petting the shoulder of a Holstein calf inside the barn, a familiar voice addressed her.

"Well, hello stranger."

She looked up to the smiling face of Gabe Murphy. Seeing her high school sweetheart sparked a flutter in her stomach. He approached and stood next to her. His features had matured into a handsome angled symmetry. Sparkling blue eyes twinkled. Tufts of dark hair peeked out and curled around his John Deere baseball cap.

Dumbfounded for a moment, she resisted an impulsive urge to wrap her arms around him like she so often did as a teenager. Instead, she clasped her hands together in front of her and stammered, "Gabe ... it's so ... so nice to see you. Imagine the thousands of people here today, and we run into each other. What are you doing here?"

"Showing some of my uncle's cows, of course," he said. That's Molly you're cuddling up to." He grinned and rubbed the calf behind her ear. His mesmerizing gaze lingered on her long enough to spark a flush of heat in her cheeks.

"So how are you?" He stepped close to her. The smell of musty sweat clung to his t-shirt that stretched across his broad chest.

Fifteen minutes later they sat on the bench outside the cattle barn, each holding an ice cream cone. The heat of the day persisted, melting the frozen scoops. Lydia licked the sticky drips from her fingers. Both laughed at the messiness, gobbling up their treats to the last satisfying bite.

Late afternoon shade from the surrounding leafy trees merged and lengthened like stretched taffy. The breeze carried the scent of fried bread and the sweetness of cotton candy. Humming crowd noise faded into an indefinite background instrumental while Gabe and Lydia chatted about the fair and farm life.

A lull in the conversation cracked with Gabe's question. "So ... how is Robert?"

Lydia's pulse quickened with surprise. "How did you know I was married?" she asked, twisting her wedding ring around her finger.

"Well," Gabe pointed to her left hand. "In addition to the big-ass diamond there, I figured you probably married the same guy that we broke up over."

"You remembered his name."

"How could I forget?"

The mention of Robert flushed guilt through her, drowning her jovial mood. She jumped up from the bench, looking at her watch.

"I'm sorry, Gabe, I have to go. I'm already late."

The pleasurable time spent with him spun into a flood of transgression.

"It's been very nice visiting with you." Clutching her purse, she turned to walk away.

"I'm sorry, Lydia, please ... wait, don't go." Gabe grasped her hand and she pivoted toward him. His tender touch ignited a sensation of electricity up her arm. An ache to linger with him clashed with her desperate urge to flee.

"I can't stay. Robert is out of town, and I have to be home when he calls."

"Will you come to see me again tomorrow? I'm staying in my trailer at the fairgrounds camp area. I'm leaving the day after tomorrow, but I'll be here in the barn most of the time. Please, come see me again." His voice changed from the previous casual tone to something deep, filled with need.

Lydia's tear-brimmed eyes fixed on his gaze. A clash of desire and guilt tore at her.

"I'm sorry, Gabe. I can't see you again." She turned and walked away.

Chapter 17

Wednesday Early Afternoon

Melissa rose from the studio chair when the doorbell rang. Doc barked and rushed to the front door. She trailed behind, descending the stairs to the door, and peered out the sidelight window. Two women, one elderly, the other younger, stood on the porch. The younger woman carried a wicker basket at her side. Melissa opened the door halfway.

The younger woman flashed a confused look when she saw Melissa. "Oh, hi, is Gabe here? We heard about Lydia and wanted to pay our respects. I brought a casserole," she said, tilting her head in the direction of the basket.

Melissa hesitated. Her instinct from years of living in the city resisted the thought of letting unannounced strangers into the house but judging from their appearance, the probability these women possessed criminal intent was low. "Yes, of course, come in," she opened the door wider and beckoned them inside.

"I'm Sherry, this is my mom, Edith." The old lady looked up through her eyeglasses at Melissa and studied her face. Her diminutive frame wobbled as she took a shaky step, grasping the younger woman's meaty upper arm. A cane balanced her other side.

"I'm Melissa, Gabe isn't here right now but I expect him back shortly. Would you like to sit down? Can I bring you lemonade or something?"

Sherry nodded, "yes, thank you."

The guests took a seat in the living room and Melissa carried the warm casserole into the kitchen and returned with a couple of glasses of lemonade.

"I'm sorry for the sudden visit," Sherry said. "I tried calling first, a little bit ago and realized I dialed Lydia's phone. Habit, you know, speed dial." Sherry shook her head and clapped her palm against her forehead. "When I realized what I did, I hung up. Are you a relative?" She asked, taking a sip of lemonade.

"Yes, I'm Lydia's daughter from her first marriage."

The old woman lifted her chin that had rested on her chest. "Where's Lydia?" She creaked.

"Mom," Sherry responded in a loud voice toward her mother's ear. "Remember, we talked about this — we wanted to visit Gabe to pay our respects because Lydia passed away."

"Lydia passed away?" The old woman looked surprised and shook her head murmuring, "So young."

Sherry made an eye roll toward her mother and looked back at Melissa. Dementia. She mouthed the word in an exaggerated gesture. Melissa nodded with a demure smile, not quite sure how to respond.

"Mom and Dad used to live down the road here aways," Sherry said. "Dad died in 2002 and mom sold the place a few years later." Sherry's rotund torso wrapped into the sofa cushions. "Now Mom lives at Green Hills, the assisted living home in town. I live down the gravel road a couple of miles from here where me and my husband farmed. My dear Charlie died a few years back. Tractor tipped on a hill and rolled over on him."

"I'm so sorry." Melissa winced at the thought of the gruesome death.

Sherry nodded. "Our family's been friends since Gabe's uncle had this farm – known Gabe since he was a youngster visiting here in the summers. He and I are just about the same age."

Melissa smiled, hoping Gabe would arrive soon to relieve her of small talk. "So, you know the visitation is tonight at the funeral home, right?"

"Oh, yeah, Sherry said, shifting in her seat. "As much as I'd like to go, I don't drive at night on the country roads. Too many deer wanderin' around. You don't wanna be driving sixty miles an hour and meet up with one of them critters crossing your path. Bobcats been seen, too."

Melissa thought about her trip here the previous night, now enlightened about the perils of travel in the country.

Edith fixed her gaze on Melissa. "Who are you?" The old woman asked in a puzzled voice.

"I'm Melissa, Lydia's daughter."

Sherry ignored her mother's befuddlement and looked at Melissa. "Lydia and I met while I was volunteering at the school. When she wasn't substitute teaching, she volunteered. Her work with the kids will really be missed. She always had art materials for every student, bought with her own money."

Melissa nodded, imagining her mom surrounded by children.

Sherry's eyes wandered around the room for a moment. "I always loved Lydia's artwork. I never was a very creative person, myself. I couldn't draw or nothin' like that, but she encouraged me to find creative things in my life. I like to cook and bake so I started making a lot of my own recipes."

She looked at Melissa and smiled. "The casserole I brought you was made from scratch with my own low-fat cream sauce."

"Thank you, Sherry, I'm sure it's delicious."

The conversation stopped when the front door opened and Gabe appeared. A wave of relief from the chit-chat brushed over Melissa.

Gabe strode over to the group of women. "Hello, neighbors," he said and bowed down toward the old woman, his face close to hers. He took her hand, "How are you, Edith?" His voice was louder than his usual tone. Edith straightened slightly from her hunched position but didn't reply, just grinned, revealing her yellowed teeth.

Sherry looked at Gabe. Her smile quickly altered to an expression of sympathy. "Mom and I just wanted to let you know how sorry we are about Lydia. She was a wonderful friend."

"Sherry brought a casserole," Melissa piped in. Their guest beamed.

"Thank you, Sherry," Gabe said. "Your apple pie at last summer's picnic sure was good."

Edith adjusted her glasses and stared at Gabe, then Melissa. Her eyes loomed large, magnified by her spectacles. "My, my, but you do look so much like your father when he was a young man." The old lady's thin voice wavered but her stare had a look of certainty as her eyes crawled back and forth between them.

Sherry blushed and turned to her mother with an exasperated sigh. "Mom, Melissa is Lydia's daughter by another marriage." Her voice boomed loud enough to be heard from another room.

Edith leaned her chin forward and narrowed her eyes, scrutinizing the pair. "Oh, yes, of course," she mumbled. Trembling fingertips hovered over thin lips. "I sometimes get a little confused."

Sherry shook her head and slapped her palms on the top of her thighs, pushing up from her seat. She placed her hand on the arm of her mother in a gesture that it was time to leave. "Well, thank you for your hospitality. We've taken up enough of your time, just wanted to give our condolences."

"Will we see you at the visitation tonight?" Gabe asked.

Sherry shuffled her feet. "I'd like to. Mom will be back home at Green Hills then. I don't like driving alone at night, so I guess not."

"Well, if that's what worries you, we can pick you up and you can ride with us," Gabe said.

Sherry smiled. "That's awfully nice of you. If it's no bother, I'd like that." She looked at Melissa who smiled back with a nod.

"I'm glad you stopped by," Gabe said, taking a step forward to assist Sherry with raising Edith from her chair and walking them to the door. "Thank you for the casserole, very kindly of you. We'll pick you up at your house tonight around 6:00."

Edith gave a tremulous look at Melissa. "I hope you feel better now, Lydia. I'll see you again soon."

Chapter 18

Wednesday Early Afternoon

After Sherry and Edith left, Melissa loaded glasses into the dishwasher and wiped the kitchen countertop. Gabe sat a few feet away at the dining room table, reading a sympathy card that had arrived in the mail. She pulled up a chair and sat across from him, resting her elbows on the table's wooden surface with interlaced fingers. "Gabe, I was wondering about something."

He looked up. "What is it?"

"While you were away today, I read Mom's second letter. Written just before you got married. She invited me to the wedding."

She chewed her lip, waiting for a reaction.

He motioned with a slight nod.

"Well, in the letter, she mentioned something important she wanted to tell me in person. Do you know what she meant by that?"

He leaned back in the chair and stroked his chin. "Hmm, did she give you any clue as to what that might be?"

She shook her head. "No, but I guess it must have been something she didn't want to state in a letter. What could have been that serious?"

"Maybe she just wanted to see you… and doubled down with her ask. If a wedding didn't convince you to come, maybe a mystery would."

Melissa straightened her shoulders. "Come on, Gabe." She leaned back, scrutinizing his face. "I realize you and I haven't known each other that long, but I believe you are an honest person. I get the feeling there's something you need to say."

He looked down at his hands, shaking his head. "You're right. There's more you need to know. You should have known much sooner, but I just didn't know how to bring it up."

"What is it? Gabe, just tell me." Her eyes widened and she placed her hand on the table as if to steady herself.

A ringing phone shattered the silence. Gabe withdrew it from his pocket and peered at the screen. A second ring persisted. He looked at her with lowered brows.

"I'm sorry, Melissa, it's my foreman. I have to get this. He held it to his ear and listened for a few seconds. "Okay, yes, I'll be right there." He hung up and flashed a worried expression she had not seen before.

"What is it? What's wrong?" She asked with alarm.

"We've got trouble in the barn." He grabbed his jacket from the back of the chair and hurried toward the door.

"What's happening?"

"Stay here. You probably won't want to see this," he said over his shoulder.

"What is it? She sprung from the chair.

"No time to explain. Stay or come, but I have to go."

Without waiting for her, he raced into the yard toward the cattle enclosures.

Melissa pulled on the muckers and grabbed her jacket, dashing outside in a sprint. A few minutes later, she stepped into the doorway of the cow barn and froze. Her chest heaved with the exertion from the run. The air held a slight antiseptic smell mixed with sawdust.

With a broad sweep of the dim interior, she tried to decipher what required such immediate attention. It didn't take long to find out.

A mammoth cow lay on her side in bedding of straw. Legs stretched out straight from her swollen belly. The poor animal looked like a giant black and white inflatable, ready to burst. Gabe stood between Melissa and the foreman who crouched behind the cow. When Gabe stepped aside, Melissa's hand shot to her mouth to suppress a retching gag. The foreman wrenched his body against the cow's back end, twisting his arm inside the cavity. He and Gabe spoke in low but animated voices. She stood several feet away, straining to hear the conversation. The foreman grimaced while his arm drilled deeper into the animal's cavity.

The beast bellowed a deep, guttural moan that sounded like a Bay Area foghorn. Her plaintive cry reached a crescendo with a high-pitched wail. Melissa felt like a pitiful bystander, unable to move.

Gabe turned and hurried back to where Melissa stood frozen in place.

"She's in labor and the calf is breech. We have to turn it around. I need the chain."

He brushed past her and returned, carrying a chain. The metal appeared similar to a bulky piece of tarnished jewelry.

Reaching out to a nearby stall, Melissa grasped a railing to steady herself. The odor of sour air contributed to her rising nausea when she took a deep breath. Her eyes fixed riveted on the scene.

The foreman withdrew his arm covered in slime and blood. He stood back and wiped his long glove with a towel as calmly as if he had just taken a dip in the nearby pond. Gabe moved in alongside the cow and donned long rubber gloves that reached past his elbows. He leaned against the animal in a braced stance. His back faced Melissa and she craned her neck to watch.

"Got the legs!" he shouted a few minutes later. He launched himself backward, clutching the bloody chain wrapped around two small, thin appendages. A pair of tiny hooves inched out, only to retreat again. His back-and-forth movement repeated with each contraction, like a fisherman reeling in an arduous catch. Situated on his backside with bent knees, he dug his heels into the packed dirt of the floor. Gabe grunted with each strenuous tug. The cow raised her head, nostrils flaring. Wide bovine eyes stared at Melissa with an intensity that sent a shiver through her. The animal's anguished cries intensified. Each groan bore more urgent than the last.

Melissa lost track of time, mired in helplessness to do anything, except perform the role of witness to the mother's agony and Gabe's efforts.

When more of the legs emerged, Gabe and the foreman's voices rose in excitement. After several more rigorous efforts from Gabe, together with the animal's shriek, the extruded calf dropped to the ground. A bloody gush of afterbirth pooled dark red across the floor. Gabe pulled the newborn alongside his crouched body. He rubbed it with a towel, using brisk motions, until the light-colored terrycloth blossomed shades of crimson. The calf lay motionless.

Melissa inched forward, straining for a closer view. "Is it all right?"

Gabe didn't answer. "Come on, baby… breathe," he whispered while clearing the nostrils and mouth of pink, slimy mucus. He raised his head toward Melissa and waved her closer. The calf squirmed. Legs thrashed in the air before it settled onto its side in a cushioned bed of straw. Gabe flashed a wide grin. "She looks like a healthy girl," he crowed. He stood and peeled off the gloves, still glistening with fluids. "Foreman can take over from here." The men exchanged nods.

Melissa covered her open mouth, suppressing the visceral urge to either throw up or cry.

Chapter 19

Wednesday Late Afternoon

After returning from the barn, Melissa tidied up, donning her black skirt and gray turtleneck in anticipation of the funeral visitation. Sherry's casserole served as a quick dinner. Gabe hurried upstairs for a shower after they ate while Melissa finished clearing dirty dishes from the dining room table. A fiery sunset hovered low on the horizon, and Melissa watched the radiant display from the kitchen window.

The calf birth had compressed their timeline. They still needed to pick up Sherry and arrive at the funeral home by 7:00 when mourners were expected to arrive. Even though she didn't relish the thought of the next few hours, she disliked being late. Nervous energy fueled her restlessness while waiting for Gabe. She hadn't forgotten their unfinished discussion just before he got the call from the foreman. Pacing into the living room, she stopped in front of the bookcase. Silly ornaments decorated the shelves. Something about them stood out to her — the kitschy ceramic leprechaun, the mother cow and calf. The lack of artistry of the ceramic and glass objects seemed out of place for someone like her mother who had studied the world of fine art. Even though her knowledge had been self-taught, the woman had an intuitive talent for capturing raw beauty in her renderings.

When Gabe descended the stairway, his appearance had

transformed from his typical casual wardrobe of jeans and baseball cap. Instead, he wore a white button-down shirt, tie, and dark blue trousers. His thick silver hair smoothed against the back of his neck, fringing over his pressed collar.

He walked over and stood next to her. "You look very nice." The compliment made her smile.

"Thanks, and you do too," she said.

He returned her smile and folded a handkerchief before tucking it into his pants pocket.

"Are you ready to go?"

Melissa shifted her stance. "I know we don't have a lot of time, but I would like to take a few minutes to talk before we go, if you don't mind."

Gabe looked at his watch and nodded. "Sure, what's going on?"

"Um," Melissa blurted out before she lost her gumption. "Can we continue the conversation we had earlier today? You know — before the —" she hesitated, searching how to describe it, "the calf thing."

His smile faded, replaced by a solemn expression. He nodded, lowering his chin. "Yes, we do have things to talk about." He stood motionless and overlapped his hands, touching his wedding band. "Have a seat. Would you care to join me for a drink?"

She nodded and settled on a chair while Gabe scurried into the kitchen and returned with two highball glasses. Ice cubes rattled when he placed the glasses on the coffee table. Lifting a bottle of bourbon in his hand, he looked at her with raised eyebrows. "Bourbon okay with you?"

"Just a short one. I'm not much of a drinker."

"Me either. Just on special occasions mostly."

The burnished liquid swirled into the glasses and its toasty fragrance released into the air. What did he define as a special occasion? The passing of a loved one? The funeral? Or something else?

He sat next to her, holding the raised glass in his hand. "To Lydia."

"To Mom." Melissa clinked his glass with hers. The first swallow heated her throat, and she wrinkled her nose.

Gabe's fingertips tapped the glass in a steady beat, his expression troubled. "Your mom had so many things she wanted to share with you, but there was always ... well, obstacles. Excuses really. Not the right time, or the right place, or the right way to do it."

Melissa burst with anticipation but refrained from interrupting his train of thought.

He took a deep breath. "You know I told you I didn't have any children?"

"Yes," she said.

"Well, I do. A daughter."

Melissa sat up straight in surprise. "Oh, okay." She drew out the words in slow motion. "When did you find out?"

"I didn't know about her until about a dozen years ago. If I had known about her sooner, my life would have been different. I would have searched for her, my only child. The one I hoped for."

Melissa blinked and cocked her head. "I'm sorry, Gabe. I'm confused. So, you have a daughter, not with your first wife, but someone else? Are you saying you cheated on my mom? Is that what she needed to tell me in person?"

"No, no. It wasn't that." He shook his head and flicked a split-second smile.

Melissa leaned closer to him. "Have you contacted your daughter? Maybe she'd want to know about you, too."

"My daughter never knew about me, either. We just recently met." He straightened his shoulders and stared at her with an intensity that caused her to hold her breath.

"Remember when I told you Lydia and I knew each other in high school?"

"Y-e-s." She wanted him to get to the point.

"And after that, the next time we saw each other was at the state fair?"

"Uh-huh," she tapped her foot in a nervous rhythm.

"That was the year 1977, the year before you were born ... more precisely, nine months before you were born." His blue eyes seared into hers.

Melissa froze, dumbfounded. The thud of her heartbeat pounded in her ears.

In a sudden flash, the figurine of the leprechaun on the shelf next to her swelled. Its comic face filled her mind's eye, as if she had just figured out the joke. The painted grin plastered across the porcelain cheeks rendered larger than proportionately reasonable. For the first time, the inscribed quip on its base fit the puzzle. Kiss Me, I'm Irish.

Her head pounded. Words Jeremy spoke on the plane echoed in her ears. Are you of Irish descent? The photo of Gabe as a young man — blue eyes, black hair, just like hers. Edith, with her muddled, yet observant, comparison of the two.

Gabe's words rushed out. "You should have been told a long time ago. Lydia hid it from everyone, even me, for all those years. When she — we — tried to find you, to tell you, but it was too late. She went to the grave with her secret."

Her jaw dropped open. She forced herself to draw a breath.

"What are you saying? That you are my ... my birth father?"

Without waiting for his answer, she shot straight up from her chair, jolted as if an electric current had just coursed through her. She stumbled away from him, rocking the chair backwards.

"I don't believe you! That's the most absurd thing I've ever heard!" Her face burned. "If that were true, how could she have hidden that from me?" The words ripped from her, flooding her brain. Stealing her balance.

"Oh my God! Does my dad know?"

A wave of dizziness overwhelmed her, and she dropped back on the chair. Her entire body shook.

"No, no, no," she repeated in a dry voice, cradling her forehead.

Gabe reached out his hand. "I'm so sorry, Melissa. Sorry you found out this way."

She recoiled away and thrust the palm of her hand straight out toward him. "Stop. Just. Stop." She pivoted and stormed out the back door.

Chapter 20

Lydia and Gabe 1977

Lydia arrived home to find the answering machine blinking its red light. Robert's recorded voice sounded annoyed.

Her throat tightened in fear. She knew he would call back and drill her like a skilled attorney confronting a witness. Only the response she held had no truthful answers.

She picked up when the phone rang again.

"Where have you been? It's 7:15. Did you get my message?" Irritation laced Robert's first words.

She brushed sweat from her forehead. "Sorry I missed your call. The traffic was terrible, and it took longer than expected to get home." That half-truth appeared to somewhat appease him when his tone flipped to an artificial sweetness.

"Well, I just worry about you and want to know where you are, honey. The project is going well, and I'll probably be home early."

"When?" Lydia asked, winding her fingers around the coiled phone cord.

"It'll be a surprise. Plus, I have some good news. I'll tell you when I get there."

After the call, Lydia pondered what good news he could possibly have. The phone rang again, and this time her mother's voice chirped in her ear.

"Lydia, I want to go to the fair with you in the morning."

"Mom, you know I have to work there, right?"

"It's fine," Ruth replied. "I'll entertain myself until you finish and then we can enjoy the fair together."

Lydia's concern was not about Ruth's entertainment. Ever since she had seen Gabe, her thoughts swirled around him. Fantasies played out in her imagination of being with him, remembering their high school days together. The feel of his muscular body next to hers made her quiver, remembering way he used to inch his fingers across her lips and trace down her neck with a sensual touch.

"Lydia, honey, are you still there?" Ruth asked.

Lydia sighed into the phone. "Sure, Mom. I'll pick you up tomorrow." Any attempt to dissuade her mother from their annual tradition would just disappoint Ruth and make them both unhappy. She tucked away thoughts of Gabe.

The next day Lydia found herself trudging around the fairgrounds with her mother. They flitted between exhibits of fabric quilts, homemade pies and jellies, and cooking demonstrations of miracle no-stick pans. What had been a pleasure for Lydia in the past now seemed burdensome. Intrusion into her time to explore at her own pace without explanation to anyone.

By late afternoon, the two women had reached the cattle barn in the corner of the fairgrounds.

"Let's go and see the largest bull," Ruth said. She grabbed Lydia's arm and plowed forward toward the barn to view the popular attraction of bovine oddities.

Lydia had spent the last couple hours avoiding this very moment. Running into Gabe would be awkward. She wouldn't be able to hide her thoughts about him from her mother. Ruth seemed to be a mind reader when it came to picking up both good and bad intentions from people.

"Mom, you're wearing me out. Let's go home." Lydia pointed away from the barn in the other direction.

"Nonsense, we're here now. This will be our last stop, okay?"

Ruth released her daughter's arm and disappeared like a mischievous child into a milling crowd of men with cowboy hats. Lydia followed. The smell of hay and manure carried in the air, pushed by fans to cool both human and animal. Maybe she could retrieve her stubborn mother and make a hasty retreat. Inside, she caught up with Ruth, who looked intrigued by a brown jersey cow munching hay in a stall.

"Mom, the line is really long to see the bull."

"Why are you being so fussy, Lydia? We're almost to the pen. We can leave after we see him. It's a tradition."

Waiting in a line, Lydia scanned in the direction of the livestock stalls where she had seen Gabe the day before. The crushing public blotted out any view within the immediate circle of people.

After marveling at the massive bull reclining inside a sprawling, fenced enclosure, Lydia breathed a sigh of relief at the success of avoiding an encounter with Gabe. She simply wanted to blend into the wall of people and disappear, not deal with any emotions seeing Gabe would conjure.

The two women strolled toward the barn exit, Lydia in the lead, setting her sight on the direction of the parking lot. When she heard Ruth say something undecipherable to her in a low voice, she turned toward her mother. Lydia's focus shifted away from Ruth and followed her line of sight. Gabe walked toward them. A smile brightened his face. That same smile Lydia had always loved. A sudden burst of heat coursed through her, one not caused from the sweltering summer temperatures.

"Well, hello ladies," he said as he touched his fingers to his ball cap in a cordial greeting. Lydia produced an uneasy smile while her heart thumped.

"My, my, is that you, Gabe?" Ruth asked with a tone of genuine surprise. "What's it been, three or four years since I've seen you?"

"Since high school. Almost five years now. How are you,

Ruth?" Gabe asked. His eyes darted from her to Lydia and back again.

"What brings you to the fair?" Ruth asked.

"I'm showing my uncle's cows. They've done well in the classes. We've won a couple ribbons and gotten a few buyers interested in our dairy products."

Ruth sniffed with an air of judgment. "That's wonderful. I'm glad the country life suits you."

Lydia broke her fixed look from Gabe to Ruth who returned her stare. She recognized her mother's scrutinizing expression.

Ruth faced Gabe and offered a polite smile. "Well, it was so nice to see you again. Lydia and I are both exhausted from walking around in this heat. We were just headed home now."

"Oh, yes, so nice seeing you," he said. "I'll be headed back home soon, too. Day after tomorrow." His eyes darted from Ruth to Lydia.

Lydia's feet sunk into the floor as if stuck in mud. She wanted to throw her arms around him and be whisked away. Instead, she squeaked out a feeble response. "Goodbye, Gabe."

A crestfallen expression crossed his face. Lydia swallowed, biting back everything she wanted to say to him. Following her mother out the exit, she realized she would never see him again.

***

The trip from the fairgrounds to home was quiet at first. The late afternoon traffic had slowed to a crawl. Carloads of weary fairgoers mixed with rush hour commuters that snaked along University Avenue.

Idling at a traffic light, Ruth broke the silence. "I suspect you'll be glad when Robert gets home. He's such a hard worker. He adores you—you know—and is so concerned about you he calls you every night while he's gone."

"Uh huh," Lydia muttered, uncomfortable to debate her

mother's assessment of her marriage. Lydia scrunched her face. "But sometimes, he acts, well, a little bit bossy."

"Nonsense. He takes charge. That's what a dependable man does," said Ruth. "A good man like Robert is hard to find. You should be grateful for that. Your husband doesn't have the excesses of most men, like smoking or drinking or gambling. He's got himself a good sense of business too. He'll take care of you. Heaven knows I wished I had more time with your dear father before he passed."

Lydia's annoyance with her mother's account of what she needed to be grateful for made her jaw clench, even though her words held some truth. "What are you getting at, Mom?" Lydia drummed her fingers on the steering wheel.

Ruth bristled. "Nothing, I'm just telling you that wedding vows are sacred. Even though marriage is sometimes hard, you should count your blessings."

Lydia sighed and punched the accelerator when the light turned green. She really had enough of her mother for the day.

***

That evening after Robert's call, Lydia soaked in the bathtub. Thoughts of Gabe flooded her. She closed her eyes, splashing her face with tepid water as if that could wash away the desire she struggled to deny. Toweling off, her skin remained dewy from the humidity as she threw on her new Iowa State Fair t-shirt, cut-off shorts, and sandals. In one impulsive moment, she grabbed her purse and strode to her car. The muggy air had not cooled outside despite the sun hovering low in the western sky.

She drove as if in a spontaneous trance, following some instinctive call. Her hurried stride through the fairgrounds became fueled by something primal.

The crowd of fairgoers had thinned to a few stragglers and workers closing exhibits for the evening. Bustling noise from the afternoon had quieted to the resonance of settling nightfall. Approaching the cattle barn, she spotted Gabe sitting alone on the bench by the entrance leafing through a booklet titled Iowa State Fair Adventures. The ball cap rested beside him, freeing his tangled waves of dark hair that cascaded around his jawline. When he raised his head, their eyes met. He stood, releasing the booklet, sending it fluttering to the ground. A perplexed expression fell across his face. Lydia drew closer and without a word took his hand, holding it for a moment, searching his blue eyes with a piercing intensity. She leaned into him and rested her head on his shoulders, inhaling his intoxicating scent, once so familiar, yet brand new. His arms circled her waist and their bodies pressed together. She exhaled a soft sigh as his lips nuzzled her ear. They embraced with urgent eagerness, the passion in his kiss ignited her entire body.

Chapter 21

Wednesday Early Evening

The last bit of daylight sank behind the horizon as Melissa launched herself outside, slamming the front door of the farmhouse. Gabe's revelation about her parentage immediately flooded her with a screaming impulse to flee. Adrenaline fueled a turbulent stew of shock, disbelief, and betrayal. She stormed down the gravel driveway.

Gabe must be deluded. Maybe he believed his fatherhood to be true because he wanted to believe it. Perhaps her mother had lied to him, knowing how much he regretted being childless. The family resemblance had to be a mere coincidence. There was no way she would believe it until proven. A DNA test would resolve his false claim and the matter would be settled.

She strode under the farmyard light perched high on a utility pole cutting through the brightness like a theatrical spotlight. The ground seemed to tremble with each pounding step as she marched through the illumination onto the darkened roadway.

A chilled breeze penetrated her lightweight sweater and curled around her bare legs. She hugged herself, rubbing her hands along her arms in a vain attempt for warmth. Stumbling along the cratered road, rocks stabbed her feet through the bottom of her thin-soled shoes and threw her off balance.

Murky clouds hid the stars, and the shroud of night hindered the speed of her steps, filling her with apprehension. She slowed her pace and peered out into the darkness. What hungry wild animals lurked nearby, just beyond view? Sherry had mentioned sightings of bobcats.

Outdoors alone in the darkness felt more oppressive than inside a San Francisco efficiency apartment during a blackout. The thought of being home right now, in civilization, back to familiar places, city lights, and sidewalks left her questioning the reason she ended up here.

Headlights cast a bright beam from a vehicle driving up behind her. She turned, wiping her runny nose on the cuff of her sleeve. The glare blinded her, and she raised a hand to shade her eyes. Gabe pulled up beside her and lowered the driver-side window. "It's a lot easier to drive to the funeral home," he said.

Melissa ignored his witticism and quickened her pace, pushing straight ahead of the car with a determined persistence. The sound of crunching gravel behind her ceased and the car door squeaked open. His approaching footsteps caused her to pause in a stubborn stance, and she glared down at the tortuous road surface. Her feet hurt and she shivered from the night air. Her arms crossed her chest. He walked up beside her.

"Look, Melissa. You wanted to know ... and needed to know. I get it that you're upset and I'm sorry about that. Telling you was never going to be easy for either of us."

She pivoted and glowered at him.

"I have this for you," he said in a steady voice, arm outstretched with a coat in hand.

She blew moist breath into the frigid air, seized the jacket, and threw it on while trudging to the car. Gabe opened the passenger door and she dropped into the leather seat. He eased in behind the steering wheel.

"I'm worried about you," he said. "Are you okay?"

She turned away from him and threw an unfocused gaze out the window. "Sure, I'm great," she huffed. "But let's not talk about it now."

***

They drove to Sherry's house in silence, arriving late.

"Thanks for the ride," Sherry said, clambering into the back seat. "I hope it's no trouble."

"No trouble at all," Gabe said, steering back to the road.

"Hello, Sherry," Melissa said with a brief glance at the neighbor and returned to staring out the window.

In a way, Sherry's presence offered a welcomed reprieve from any difficult discussions looming with Gabe. Melissa's tension diminished and she relaxed into the seat. A polite conversation could fill the awkward void.

"I'm really goin' to miss Lydia," Sherry said. "She was a good person, a good listener too. I talk a lot, so maybe that's the reason we became friends. Opposites attract like they say."

Gabe turned the Ford sedan onto the highway toward town.

"I just can't imagine what it's like losing a mother. I've had Mom around all my life. She helped me raise my three boys and did farm work too. I don't know how I would have managed it all without her. Don't get me wrong, we've had disagreements, but we don't stay mad for long. It's especially hard watching her lose her memory. She remembers things from long ago but can't remember what she ate for breakfast just an hour earlier."

"Lydia liked your mom," Gabe said. "Edith reminded her of Ruth and taught her a lot about living the country life."

A light rain began, and sprinkles dotted the windshield. The conversation lulled with only the mechanical cadence of wipers slapping back and forth.

Sherry leaned forward toward Melissa. "I've been thinking about Lydia a lot and our visits together. I don't recall her talking about having a daughter."

"Yeah, my mom was quiet about a lot of things."

"Well, that's pretty typical around here. Kids leave for the cities. Don't wanna work on the farm or stay in their small town.

Folks left here don't like talkin' about their kids that don't wanna come visit. So, everyone just tries to mind their own business. Heaven knows, we got enough to worry about. Summers hot as hell and winter freezes so cold tears stick to your face like icicles. And then a goddamn tornado can blow everything down in a minute." She hesitated for a breath." Pardon my French."

Melissa leaned her head against the passenger window. The rain dripped animated rivulets on the glass, creating a hypnotic effect. The passing landscape blurred into wavering tones of charcoal and ebony. Sherry's monotone voice added to the drowsy rhythm.

Sherry took a long breath. "But then, you know, there will be days just like heaven. Perfect weather, a gentle breeze carries the smell of fresh air over the hills. You eat green beans and tomatoes picked out of your own garden or a trout you just caught straight from the stream."

"Yeah, and the best sweet corn on the planet in your backyard," Gabe piped in.

Sherry's voice perked up. "Gets you thinkin' life ain't so bad. There's lots to be grateful for, it's just a matter of lookin' at things with a different perspective."

***

The drizzle had stopped by the time they arrived at Wilson's Funeral Home. The vintage three-story building struck Melissa as an odd combination of architecture, with patches of modern updates around the windows and steps. The sagging exterior of a once glorious nineteenth-century Victorian home appeared foreboding in the dark. A fitting movie set for a spooky film.

A separate one-story structure adjacent to the home displayed a sign that read Reception Hall with an arrow pointing to its entrance. Gabe led the way past the sign toward the main building. He held the large, glass door open for the women.

A man in a dark suit introduced himself inside the entrance foyer and directed them to a drawing-room doorway. A sign posted on an easel held a photo of Lydia and the name Murphy underneath.

Mid-century modern decor furnished the large room. Porcelain table lamps sprinkled throughout provided soft lighting around furniture groupings of straight-back wooden chairs with upholstered seats. A cloying scent of lilies hung in the air like stale perfume. The space reminded Melissa of Grandma Ruth's living room, only on a larger scale. The burnished wooden coffin in the recessed alcove provided a striking disparity to the homey environment.

Hushed conversations from the twenty or so people in the room quieted as Gabe and Melissa entered. The somber tune of recorded Celtic harp and flute issued from the music system. A few guests hovered close to the flower arrangements spaced around the front of the room. Others were seated in the rows of Eames-style chairs that faced forward to the coffin.

Sherry turned to Melissa and reached for her hand, patting it with a gentle touch.

"I know this is very hard for you, hon." She reached for a tissue from a box on the nearby credenza and placed it in Melissa's hand.

Melissa nodded and offered a weak smile. Her mind numbed, frozen into a block of ice, movements simply mechanical functions. She wanted to run back to the car and lock herself inside but couldn't budge. The warmth of Gabe's hand on her back did little to comfort her.

"I'll help greet people," Sherry said looking assured with her self-assigned task. She surveyed the room, then back at Gabe. "There's some folks I know over there." She strode toward a small group of people standing in a corner.

Gabe leaned toward Melissa and whispered in her ear. "Will you be okay?"

She snapped out of her stupor. "Yes, of course," she said and lifted her chin.

Years spent dealing with clients taught her the necessity to project a cordial expression, regardless of mood. At this moment, however, her face hardened like dried clay, jaw clenched.

"I can introduce you to people here." Gabe gestured toward the gathering.

"Not right now, Gabe. Just give me a minute." She inhaled and attempted a smile. "You don't need to hover. I can manage myself. Go ahead and connect with your friends." The remark intended to sound confident but came across as arrogant.

He patted her arm and pivoted toward two men standing nearby. Squelching her discomfort, she wandered toward an impressive floral spray, studying the arrangement of yellow chrysanthemums nestled alongside twisted branches.

A voice behind her said her name.

Melissa spun around to see a woman with short-cropped dark hair wearing Gucci eyeglasses. Melissa guessed her to be in her early fifties.

"Hello, you're Melissa, aren't you?"

Melissa nodded and cocked her head in surprise this stranger would know her name.

"Do you know who I am?" the woman asked.

"No, I'm sorry, umm, have we met before?"

The woman smiled. "My name is Angela."

Chapter 22

Wednesday Evening

"I'm Angela Diaz," the woman said, grasping Melissa's hand in a firm handshake. Her touch felt velvety. Nude fingernails were clipped with perfect symmetry.

Melissa studied her for a moment. Angela's tan complexion glowed. A few wrinkles pressed into the smooth skin around her bright eyes. Dark hair framed her oval face.

"I recognize you from a photo Lydia kept. Of course, you were a teenager then."

"Yes. Gabe said you knew my mother," Melissa said, releasing her grip.

Cautious apprehension about this woman stilted Melissa's greeting. After the divorce, Robert described Lydia's girlfriend as a woman with an agenda, conniving and not to be trusted. Lydia's letter, however, depicted a rescuer and close friend.

"Gabe had called me and left a message about her passing. I almost skipped over it but realized it was from her phone number," Angela said.

"Yes, he told me you planned on attending." Melissa stopped short, ignoring the feeling she needed to be overly polite. In any other circumstance of introductions, she would likely offer a more cordial response like, nice to meet you. The sentiment and the words failed her at this moment. Robert's woeful tale played in her head. He never mentioned the name of the woman her mother ran away to live with. Only epithets and bitter words about the vile home wrecker who split up the family. The woman he would never forgive.

Angela's intense gaze penetrated Melissa. Glasses framed eyes that shimmered from hazel to brown. Thick lashes lined her lids although she wore little, if any, makeup.

"I'm so sorry for the loss of your mother. How are you doing?" Angela said.

Melissa shrugged. "I'm doing okay." She suppressed the urge to go into any depth about her range of emotions within the last few days, preferring a restrained impression of equanimity.

Questions she wanted to ask raced through her thoughts, tumbled together, and stuck in her throat.

"Is it alright if we sit for a while?" Angela asked, motioning away from the buzzing activity.

Melissa pressed her lips into a thin line and glanced around the room, spotting Gabe engrossed in conversation with a small group of people. Something about Angela's demeanor drew her in. How much did this woman really know about the estrangement? What had her mother shared and what secrets remained hidden?

"Of course," Melissa replied.

The two women retreated to chairs in a quiet corner of the room, sitting side-by-side. Angela exuded a faint scent of warm spice.

"Her passing was a shock," Angela said dabbing a tissue to the corner of her tearful eyes. Her voice wavered. "I had just called her a few months ago. We kept in touch when we could." She paused and added in a soft voice, "She missed you."

Melissa bit her lip and looked down at her hands folded on her lap. Her grip tightened into a fist and released.

Angela inhaled and her voice lifted. "Gabe said you live in San Francisco and you're self-employed in the marketing field."

"Yes, I went to college in California and stayed there after graduation. I do market research for corporate clients."

"Ah," Angela nodded. "I've always admired that skill. The ability to decipher vague and disparate data and come up with solutions. I imagine your father is very proud of you."

The reference to her father caused Melissa to flinch and look away. She hesitated to respond, questioning which father Angela referred to. "I suppose he's proud of me. I haven't kept in touch much with him since he moved to Italy."

Angela's eyebrows raised. "With Tammy, the neighbor?"

"No, that was his second wife. They divorced and he married Francesca. They met on a Mediterranean cruise and next thing I knew he had moved somewhere in Italy where she lived."

Angela nodded. Her expression showed no surprise. "Does he know about your mom's passing?"

"Yes," Melissa stated in a flat tone. She narrowed her eyes at Angela. "Mom wrote about you in a letter to me… that she had known you a long time. Funny she never mentioned you to me. I never knew your name until Gabe told me. If you were so close, why didn't I know about you?"

Angela cocked her head, "You don't remember the time we met, do you?"

Melissa squinted, combing through her memory. "I'm not sure. I have a fuzzy recollection of coming home early from school one day. Mom sat at the dining room table with a stranger."

Angela nodded.

"At the time I thought it was very unusual for her to have company. We may have been introduced, but I don't remember a name. I didn't hang around. After dinner, I asked Mom about it."

Angela folded her hands across her lap, "What did she say?"

"She said you were a coworker. You were there about some work-related thing. I didn't think anymore about it."

"That's true," Angela said. "Lydia and I became close friends when we worked together at the Art Guild. I was careful about visiting her at home, though. We'd go to lunch on workdays but never spent time together after hours."

"Why not after hours?"

Angela's expression tightened. "Robert kept track of everywhere she went and who she associated with. He didn't like her to have other attachments or be somewhere he didn't know about. He insisted friends weren't important and family should be her center of attention."

Melissa recalled her father's gift of a mobile phone at college graduation. They had joked about how he could keep better track of her now, being concerned with her safety in the big city.

Angela looked downward and shook her head. "Friendships became forbidden unless he approved, which of course, he never did. He just barely tolerated her time spent with Ruth. He dominated the relationship. She tried hard not to stir his anger."

Angela's harsh account of her dad made her uncomfortable. Melissa squelched the reaction to defend her father's side of the story. Instead, she wanted more of what Angela had to say.

"Did she ever talk about me?" Melissa said.

"Oh, yes. Mostly she regretted the sudden way she left. She lacked the confidence to take you. Her life turned upside down and she didn't know how to cope."

Melissa frowned. "But she never got in touch with me afterward. Not even a phone call." Heat rose in her cheeks.

Angela twisted toward her, touching her groomed fingertips on Melissa's wrist. "She tried several times to contact you, but obstacles always defeated her. We came to the house looking for you, despite her fear of Robert and what he might do. By the time she dared to face him, you were gone. Robert claimed he didn't know where you were. She knew it was a lie but couldn't force him to tell her the truth. After that, she lost hope."

Melissa lifted her chin and stared in the direction of the casket. Angela's tale sounded similar to Gabe's. She held doubts about Gabe's account because he could have been deceived by her mother into believing her story. But Angela had been with her mother then. She had lived through it with her.

"Surely, there were other ways to find me," Melissa persisted.

Angela shook her head. "She tried contacting the in-laws, but nobody would speak to her except to let her know they didn't want to get involved. It wasn't until much later when your Aunt Irene finally gave her an address. Searching for people then was harder than it is now."

Gabe broke away from the group he had been chatting with and approached them.

"Hello, Angela. We finally meet at last. You look just like your photo."

Angela and Melissa rose from the chairs. Angela greeted him with a handshake.

"Yes, it's too bad we meet under these circumstances. I'm so sorry about Lydia."

"Well, thank you for being here," he said.

"Coincidentally, I was in Chicago on business when you called," she said looking at Gabe. "So close by that I rented a car to drive here. I had always intended to visit, but excuses got in the way... workload or family demands. It's easy to push aside plans, thinking we have plenty of time to do it later."

Gabe nodded. "Where are you staying?"

"At the hotel in town. I'll drive to Chicago tomorrow afternoon and catch a flight back home to Miami."

"Will you be at the funeral tomorrow?" Melissa asked. She wanted more time to seek answers.

"I'll try to make it to the funeral tomorrow, but there are some work issues that need attention. I have an online meeting later tonight with my team."

The conversation quieted as Sherry approached and introduced herself to Angela.

"The prayer service will start soon," Sherry said. "Would you like to sit next to me, Angela?"

Angela nodded. "Yes, thank you."

"We'll be right behind you," Sherry said to Gabe.

Gabe turned to Melissa. "Would you care to come with me to say goodbye?" He offered his arm to her and turned his head in the direction of the alcove. She followed his gaze.

The polished, dark wood casket loomed large in the recessed space bordered by flower arrangements. Edges of Melissa's vision blurred as she and Gabe walked the aisle between the seated mourners. She focused on gathering the courage to view the remains cradled atop the bed of white satin. The finality of this moment sucked the air from her lungs. Thoughts of her mother had always been couched in terms of leaving. Deserting. Now she must accept the permanent abandonment in death.

She took a deep inhale to steel herself and wrapped a trembling hand around Gabe's arm. Any energy she had before this moment drained away. Her legs wobbled as if her bones had been replaced by straw.

Melissa hesitated as she neared the casket, focusing on the large spray of white lilies, pink carnations, and magenta roses that contrasted against the dark grain of the coffin. She looked at the sunken face of her mother and grimaced.

The body did not resemble anything about the mother she remembered. It appeared waxen, fashioned from polymer and papier-mache, sprayed with opaque pigment of pink and tan, and framed with smoothed gray hair. Thin hands lay reposed just above her waistline. Underneath the fingertips rested a snapshot of Gabe and Lydia at a younger age — he in a tux and she in the same dress that became her shroud. A photographic record of true love possessed and carried beyond this world. The absence of Melissa's image shouted of opportunities missed. Celebrations and happy times enjoyed by other mothers and daughters rang vacant in Melissa's memory.

She squeezed her eyes shut. Her shoulders hunched. This woman brought her into the world. They shared mortal bonds woven together with inextricable threads. Yet she barely knew her mother.

Her jaw clenched, battling an internal tempest of contempt and need. What other unknown secrets did her mother hold? Answers to questions Melissa longed for, destined to be interned forever. She tightened her fist around the crumpled tissue, bringing it to her face but had no tears to wipe away.

Sherry moved beside her, laying a hand on her back. "So hard to lose a mother. You must have loved her very much."

Chapter 23

Thursday Late Morning

Gabe and Melissa stood under the canopy that shaded the freshly dug ground at the cemetery. The scattering of mourners had dispersed toward their vehicles parked alongside the narrow road that traversed the grounds.

"It was a nice ceremony this morning," Gabe said in a somber voice. His gaze fell on the casket suspended by webbed straps above the cavity. He wiped a handkerchief under his glasses and stuffed it back into his pocket.

A sense of relief filled Melissa. She accomplished getting through the uncomfortable ritual. "Yes, very nice," she said in a low voice.

The funeral service an hour earlier had lasted only thirty minutes. An organ rendition of Dust in the Wind played on hidden speakers, followed by a drawn-out eulogy from the pastor about Lydia's virtues. Melissa found it hard to focus on his words, her emotional energy drained. Unlike the previous evening of the visitation, the casket remained closed, much to her relief. She hated the thought of her mother's corpse in slow decay. Her ghost hovering among the handful of attendees.

At one point, Gabe had stood at the podium in the funeral home by the casket and spoke for a few minutes until his voice cracked, his distress visible. The pastor stepped next to him with a reassuring hand on his quaking shoulder and offered an unheard whisper in his ear. Melissa closed her eyes, unable to bear witness to the misery.

After the casket had been whisked away to the cemetery, she and Gabe settled into the back seat of the family limo provided by the funeral home. The brief drive across the street to the final resting place provided more tradition than necessity.

Angela had been absent at the funeral.

"Are you ready to go to the luncheon at the funeral home?" Gabe asked when they remained alone at the gravesite. "There's sandwiches and desserts in the reception room. I feel I need to be there for the guests."

The thought of eating made her stressed gut roil. Why did the consumption of food become the standard expectation at the conclusion of ceremonial events?

"Not yet. I'm not very hungry. It's such a short walk, I'll meet you there later. I just need a little extra time. You go ahead."

Gabe nodded, laying the palm of his hand on her shoulder. He lingered for a moment, then turned and walked toward the limo where the driver waited. Melissa watched him leave. His posture sagged. Each step labored, as if bearing the heavy weight of grief.

Sitting alone under the canopy, a cool breeze brushed her face carrying the organic scent of churned dirt and roses. A white dove perched on a nearby shrub took flight and glided away. She imagined a century of secrets buried in this placid resting place, sequestered beneath the earth, forever forgotten.

Melissa withdrew her phone from her pocket to check the time. An alert flashed across the screen. Jeremy had left a message. She turned off the silent mode and opened the text.

> Hey Melissa,
> I didn't know if you got my text. Uh, well, I'd like to get together sometime. I hope you don't think I'm being too pushy. I'd like to get to know you but I understand if you ... well, if you're not interested. So, I hope everything is okay with you and your mom.

I'd like to hear from you. If not, I'll stop bothering you with these messages. Call me when you can.

Melissa held the phone and closed her eyes, composing her response. She admired his persistence. Looking back to the screen, she typed a reply.

Hi Jeremy, thanks for your messages. I don't want to give you the impression ...

She stopped when she heard a nearby car slowing, and turned to see a red Mercedes pulling to the curb.

The latecomer, dressed in a dark, tailored suit, emerged from the driver's side of the sedan, and walked toward the gravesite. Melissa squinted as the figure approached. Each step taken showed someone who possessed confidence and poise. Short black hair fluttered around her face. When the woman removed her large sunglasses, Melissa recognized Angela.

"I'm sorry I couldn't make the funeral but hoped I wasn't too late to catch you before I left," Angela said. She approached and sat next to Melissa.

"I didn't think I'd see you again," Melissa said, stowing her phone into her pocket. Her reply to Jeremy could wait. "Gabe is at the reception at the funeral home. They're serving lunch. I'm sure you'd still be able to grab a bite."

Angela shook her head. "I wanted to see you before I have to leave." Her lips parted as if she intended to say something but stopped. Her mouth turned downward.

Melissa studied her face. "Were you about to say something?"

A campanile bell at the center of the cemetery chimed with a single tone. Its mournful resonance rippled across the grounds, disrupting the stillness of the air.

The echo faded and Angela pursed her lips, brows lowered. "I owe it to Lydia to tell you the entire story. It may help you understand what happened when she left you."

"I doubt any information you have would change much for me, Angela."

"There are some things I think it's important for you to know."

"What kind of things?"

Angela gathered her breath. "Lydia had never intended to abandon the family. I'm the one that convinced her to leave."

The abrupt announcement startled Melissa but didn't surprise her. She took a moment to ponder Angela's confession. "I'm aware of that. Dad didn't want her to have friends, so she left." Angela's persistence sparked Melissa's fire to skip formalities and polite platitudes, to dig into this woman's story, unabashed and raw. "Mom traded her family for friends, or should I say, friend?" Her eyes narrowed. "I heard all about what happened from Dad. He called you a homewrecker."

Angela looked straight ahead and fixed her gaze in the distance before inhaling a deep breath. "I'm sure he saw me that way. I don't blame you for believing that. You only had the information he wanted you to hear."

"So tell me, Angela. What's your side of the story?"

Angela shook her head, looked at the casket ready for internment, and back to Melissa. "I don't know how much of the emotional abuse you may have seen between your parents, but it was much worse than you probably knew."

Melissa shifted in her chair. The words emotional abuse stung her. Her parents never really seemed very happy together. They were either arguing or not talking at all.

"Isn't that how marriage works? Couples disagree," Melissa said with a slight indignant tone.

Angela snorted and shook her head. "It's more than disagreements. Abuse is insidious. It accumulates like drips in a bucket, finally reaching a point when the bucket can't hold anymore. Lydia's acceptance of Robert's mistreatment became normal for her." Angela stared into Melissa's eyes. "Normal for you."

Melissa crossed her arms and frowned. "How do you know all this?"

Angela's face scrunched. "One day while Lydia and I had lunch together in the park she opened up and told me about how miserable she felt about herself. She doubted her ability to hold onto her job for very long because she lacked any kind of confidence. I could see she was really depressed. When she told me about Robert's behavior, I thought she probably exaggerated or perhaps was too sensitive. It wasn't like he beat her or anything." Angela hesitated before continuing. "Then I witnessed Robert's explosive anger myself."

"What? When?" Melissa's voice raised in surprise.

Angela interlaced her fingers and rested her hands in her lap for a moment before speaking. "It was late March, the same year she left and moved in with me. Lydia and I traveled to Omaha one weekend. I signed up to run a marathon there and she agreed to be my support person. It was a brave move for her to take. She had told Robert she wanted to go. Of course, he forbade it and shut down any discussion. For her to carry through with it was an act of defiance."

Melissa frowned. She didn't remember this but didn't interrupt.

Angela seemed to read her confusion. "It was a weekend when you were at your friend's house for a slumber party. Your mom and I spent a day and overnight together. Afterwards, I dropped her off at her home and Robert was there, waiting outside. He looked angry. I stayed in the car and watched. I was worried about her. She was barely at the front door when he grabbed her arm. He pulled her inside the house, ignoring me as if I weren't there. That's when the yelling started. He screamed so loud I could hear him inside my car from the driveway. He called her all kinds of horrible names. I was so shocked I wasn't sure what to do. I just sat there dumbfounded. When the yelling stopped, I got scared something bad had happened. I ran to the door and listened. I heard the back door slam, so I snuck inside, not sure what I'd find." Angela stopped and rubbed her fingers back and forth across her eyelids.

Melissa bit her lip. The fact that this woman seemed to know more about her family's dysfunction than she did, struck a nerve. She didn't want to hear it. Didn't want the unwelcome growing sense of shame that clutched her.

"Why are you telling me all this?" Melissa demanded in a sour voice.

Angela appeared unfazed by the harshness of her tone. "Maybe it's because I saw how Lydia suffered from the loss of her family. Or because I wished my own mother would have accepted me the way I am. I know what rejection and estrangement feel like. It took me a long time and much soul-searching to forgive my own mother. This is the one last thing I can do for Lydia. To share what I've learned with you."

Melissa rose, her back toward Angela. She rubbed her face with a trembling hand.

"I'm sorry, I assumed you'd want to know. I'll stop if you want," Angela said.

Melissa stared at the casket. The scent of the funeral flowers lingered sickening sweet in the air. All these years she wanted to know the truth of why her mom left. Now the opportunity arose to get a glimpse into the past. She turned to face Angela. "I'm sorry, it's a lot to take in. Please ... go on."

"Are you sure?" Angela asked.

Melissa nodded. "Yes. What happened after you went inside?"

"I found her crumpled on the floor crying, rubbing her arm." A pained look crossed Angela's face. "Robert was nowhere to be seen. I pleaded with her to come home with me right then, but she convinced me she was okay and would handle it. You weren't home and she wanted to be there when you arrived since she didn't trust Robert to be calmed down by then. So, after her reassurance, and despite my better judgment, I just left."

Melissa's jaw tightened as she tried to swallow the scenario

Angela portrayed. She had seen her parents go for days without speaking or caught her mother sometimes crying alone in the house. Several times she heard her parents argue, but not as alarming as Angela's tale.

"I find that hard to believe, Angela. I mean, he was never like that to me."

"That's why when she finally did leave, she didn't take you, because she thought you would be okay. It would be easier for you to adjust if you weren't uprooted from your home."

Melissa thought about the aftermath of the long days without her mother, seeking solace in her room. Moments of comfort in the familiar surroundings, despite the gaping emptiness of her mother's absence.

"She believed, rightly or wrongly, that Robert was a lousy husband, but a good father and would never hurt you," Angela said. "You were almost eighteen, a few weeks away from legally being an adult and ready for college. There would be no issue of custody. It took all her courage she had to finally make that decision. She wanted to keep a relationship with you."

Melissa tried to fit the pieces together from her memory that would make sense of Angela's story. She dug her fingernails into her clenched palms trying to digest what she just heard. Several seconds passed before she spoke, her words bitter. An impulse like a dam releasing a torrent of water spilled out from Melissa. The statement flowed unfettered.

"So, she went to live with you. Abandon me. Forsake the family to live a lesbian life with her lover."

Chapter 24

Thursday Late Morning

The breeze cooled under the tented canopy. Melissa's pointed statement to Angela hung in the air, daring to be addressed.

"You two were more than friends," Melissa said. "You had a lesbian affair. That's the real reason she left, wasn't it, Angela?" Her voice was terse.

Angela leaned back and looked at Melissa with raised eyebrows, "Well, you're certainly straightforward."

Melissa took a breath, aware the brusque remark sounded rude. "I'm sorry ... it's just ... that's what Dad told me on the phone yesterday. He said Mom left because of the affair."

Angela thrust her chin out with a hint of a smile. "It's okay. I appreciate someone who doesn't mince words. I'm like that too, so I'll be completely candid with you. I am a lesbian. I was always open about it with Lydia from the very beginning of our friendship. I'm not ashamed of it, nor of how we felt toward each other."

Melissa took a moment to absorb what she just heard. "But ... were you lovers?"

Angela's eyes drilled into Melissa. "Yes, but not right away. As our friendship deepened, we wanted to be together, and the relationship evolved."

Melissa cringed. She didn't want to picture her mom as anything other than the role she held as a mother. A same-sex partner presented even more quandaries.

"We were a couple in every way, slept in the same bed, and yes, we experimented sexually. But the physical part wasn't sustainable. For her anyway. Lydia questioned her lack of fulfillment in her marriage. She reached a point where men had disappointed her, and she searched for the reason. But she was far from being a lesbian."

Melissa bit her lip. Angela's story seemed so foreign. She couldn't imagine this portrayal of the mother she knew, so bold and experimental.

"But why you? Why did she run to you and abandon me?" Melissa frowned.

Angela shrugged. "I suppose she felt there were few options for her. She knew she had to leave the marriage and I provided a safe haven. It was a journey she had to discover on her own, without you."

"How did the two of you get by financially? She had no job or income then," Melissa said.

"I convinced her to come and live with me. Her dependence on Robert paralyzed her. I had strong feelings for her. I needed to save her, I guess. We weren't concerned about money."

"It must have been a struggle for you both," Melissa said.

Angela nodded. "The first year I supported her from my job at the ad agency where I worked. That was years before I started my own business. The court ordered Robert to pay a lump sum to her, instead of alimony, when the divorce became final. He always insisted it was his money, he earned it, and she would not get any of it. She was so naive, she believed him. Thankfully, I had a lawyer friend who helped her."

The thought of her father arguing over money didn't surprise Melissa. As a teenager, she often saw him negotiating with salespeople to get the cheapest price. His bargaining embarrassed her. Although he seemed preoccupied with money, he seldom talked about financial situations, and she never asked.

"Was the money from the divorce enough for her to live on?"

"It was a start. She wasn't even sure how to open a bank account when she came to live with me. I remember when the settlement check arrived, she told me it was the first time she felt independent. Her confidence grew and she found a job as an office assistant during the day and attended college classes in the evenings. Did you know she became an art teacher?"

"Yes, Gabe told me." Melissa imagined her mother in a classroom, heaping concern and affection on the children of strangers.

"I know it must be difficult to understand our relationship, Melissa." Angela gazed straight ahead over the green expanse of the cemetery. "Those three years we lived together were some of my best memories. We were happy. Part of the success of our relationship was a bond of trust, something lacking in her marriage. Lydia was 15 years older than me, but our generational difference never mattered. We healed each other with love. I think I helped her with restoring her sense of self-confidence, and she helped me come to terms with the absence of my own mother. We supported each other, without the patriarchal influence of a man."

"But you don't know what it was like for me, Angela. Those first few years I missed her so much. I thought it was my fault she left." Melissa's chin quivered.

Angela shook her head. "It wasn't your fault, Melissa. Lydia wanted a relationship with you. Timing, circumstances, and misunderstandings interfered."

Melissa took a deep inhale to steady her voice. "It sounds like you were happy with your lives. Why did you separate?"

Angela smiled. "We were best friends, contrary to the misguided belief that lesbians can't have female relationships that aren't sexual. But friendship can only be fulfilling in a limited respect. I needed to find a partner who I could share intimacy with. Maybe even get married. I found that woman who is my wife now. Your mom started on her journey toward happiness and independence. It was destined to happen. The two of us followed different paths."

"Did you ever tell your parents about your relationship?" Melissa asked.

A look of sadness crossed Angela's face. "I think I can relate to some of what you may feel about being abandoned," Angela said. "I was estranged from my mother too. Her choice, not mine. Lydia wanted a relationship with you. My mother completely rejected me."

"Why? Because you were gay?"

Angela nodded. "I came out when I was about 16. My mother and father were very conservative and couldn't deal with it. They thought it was a choice, a lifestyle to be gay like I could just go to a doctor and get it fixed. When they threatened to send me to a camp run by a religious group that claimed they could cure homosexuality, I ran away. The group reportedly used aversion therapy to produce results."

Melissa winced. One of her psychology classes in college described the controversial therapy used to control sexual urges. But the techniques seemed more akin to torture and brainwashing than anything therapeutic.

"Where did you go when you ran away?"

"I survived on the streets for a while until a friend from school talked her parents into letting me live with them. My parents gave up and agreed. My new family owned a gym and hired me to help. That's where I gained interest in business. I worked hard to finish high school, and then college. I got employment in advertising until eventually I started my ad agency."

Melissa admired Angela's strength to endure outright rejection by both parents and her determination to succeed. But that didn't mean she was prepared to fully embrace the role she played in Lydia's decision. "Did you ever reconcile with your parents?"

Angela scrunched up her face, her dark eyebrows lowered. "My mother was especially affected and never came to terms with it before she died a few years ago. Since then, my father and

I have begun a dialog, but it's strained." Her dark eyes glistened, and she curled her fingers over her mouth. "Lydia meant so much to me. Now I've lost her too."

The look of sorrow on her face needled Melissa's guilt about her lack of tears. In the brief timespan of her visit to Iowa, she had witnessed the grief of others, while she felt numb. As if her emotions drained away, encapsulated within a protective casing. Although the previous days seemed like a roller coaster of awakened feelings to her, she had not released the depths of anguish perhaps others may have expected from her. She never thought of herself as hard-hearted, just pragmatic. Too much emotional display, especially around people she didn't know, felt unseemly. But at this moment she pressed herself to subdue sentiment about Angela's reactions…and her own.

She wanted to keep an open mind. A woman seeking comfort from another woman was understandable. There were times when she commiserated with her female friends, especially after her divorce, but that was different than diving into an extramarital affair like her mother had done.

Acquaintances she met in San Francisco who were gay produced no particular judgment on her part about their relationship preferences. But the fact remained that her mother chose another life away from her daughter. She didn't begrudge her mother's happiness. It's just that it came at the expense of her own.

A melodic tone sounded from within Angela's blazer pocket. She retrieved a phone and looked at its message. "The airline is confirming my check-in for the flight back to Miami tomorrow. My wife is planning a getaway together, so I have to be back for that."

Both women stood and faced each other. Angela wrapped her arms around Melissa, pulling her close in a gentle hug. The embrace caused Melissa to stiffen from the unexpected closeness. Angela's shoulders and arms proved slender but muscular, and she smelled of orange blossoms.

"Your mom always loved you," Angela whispered.

Stepping back, Angela rested both hands on Melissa's upper arms, her touch light but firm. "I wanted to be here to pay my respects and meet you. Lydia would have liked that. She was an extraordinary woman, you know." Turning toward the coffin, she blew a kiss. Observing the motion, Melissa turned her head, uneasy with the affectionate gesture.

After a moment, Angela pivoted toward Melissa. "Please let me know if there is anything you need." She reached into her pocket, pulled out a business card and held it outward. "Really. Anything at all."

"Thank you, Angela, of course," Melissa said in a polite voice. She held the card for a moment before dropping it into her bag.

"Do you need a ride?" Angela asked before turning toward her car.

"No thanks, I want to walk." Melissa chewed her lip as she watched Angela glide away, feeling her turmoil swell. This woman's account only confirmed Melissa's belief that as a teenager, while she struggled to make sense of her pain of rejection, her mother had happily unburdened herself from the family to frolic in the discovery of the meaning of life.

Chapter 25

Lydia and Gabe 1977

Lydia opened her eyes as the pink light of dawn hovered across her face. She lay next to Gabe on the airbed of his truck camper. Their naked bodies spooned together with his arms around her waist. Rhythmic breathing and the coo of a mourning dove orchestrated into a tranquil harmony. The smell of fresh-cut grass drifted in from the small camper window.

She wanted to savor this moment and cling to last night's passion. To wake every morning with him next to her. Guilt invaded her daydream and she rolled on her back, brushing it away, dampening its sourness for just a while longer.

"Good morning, Sunshine," Gabe said, snuggling his face into the crook of her neck. His warm breath tickled her. She faced him, coiling a lock of his dark hair around her finger.

"How many times did we imagine this when we were in high school?" Gabe asked, tracing his fingertip along the rim of her ear, following her jaw to her neck.

"If I recall, we did more than imagine," she giggled.

Gabe had been a skinny teenager then. Last night she discovered a man who had matured well into his toned body. His broad shoulders and arms rippled with muscle. Taunt skin wrapped legs that once resembled sticks, now tree trunks.

"You were my first love," she said.

"And you mine." He kissed her neck, his lips lingered against her skin.

Lydia smiled. "I remember at first sex seemed awkward and messy. I wondered why everyone made such a fuss about it."

"We didn't know what we were doing then," Gabe said with a sheepish grin.

Lydia blushed. "Last night was beautiful, Gabe. More than I ever imagined it could be." She shifted onto her stomach facing him, resting her chin in her hands. Her smile faded. "What do we do now?"

"Well, there's a tractor show at the grandstand at noon today," Gabe grinned.

Lydia rolled her eyes and nudged him with her elbow. "Gabe, you know what I mean." A pout crossed her face. "About this — about us," she said biting her lower lip.

Gabe sat up and leaned against the headboard. "What I think you're asking is…will this be a one-night stand or the beginning of something more?" He wrapped his arm around her. She nodded and snuggled her head against his chest.

Stillness surrounded them, thick with possibilities. She anticipated his profession of love, followed by pleading with her to leave everything and come away with him. The flush of teenage yearning filled her with thoughts of living her life with someone she had meant to be with. At that moment, she would have gone with him anywhere.

He brushed his hand gently between her shoulder blades down to the small of her back. The morning sunshine streamed into their cocooned space as he drew the blanket around them. "Lydia, I should have told you this sooner, but … " he hesitated.

"What is it, Gabe?" His tone caused her to hold her breath in preparation for something she may not want to hear.

Gabe frowned. His previous lighthearted demeanor turned serious. "I'm so sorry, but … I'm engaged to be married."

The words stabbed her like a hot knife. A thick sensation caught in her throat. She pushed away from him and sat upright, unable to speak.

"Her name is Beth." His words rushed out. "She is a local girl...lives on the farm nearby that had been in her family for generations. I've known her for a while. We just got engaged a few months ago."

Lydia swallowed hard. The fantasy playing in her head of slow dancing with Gabe under a star-filled night dissolved into a million droplets. Her voice trembled. "Do you love her?"

Gabe paused before answering. "Yes, I do."

Her throat tightened. The trailer walls pressed inward, sucking out oxygen. How could she be so foolish? Not even thinking to ask him if he was in a relationship? But how could she judge him? She was the married one, the one who broke marriage vows. The roar of guilt returned. Springing up, she spied her panties and bra among their mingled clothing strewn on the floor. She slipped into the underwear with swift efficiency.

Gabe reached out and took her hand. "Wait, Lydia. Please."

She stopped and turned toward him. His burdened expression held a tenderness that cooled the growing heat in her chest. Mesmerizing blue eyes drew her in.

His voice wavered. "I'm so sorry. When I saw you again, I just didn't think about anything else. I never forgot about you ... about wanting you."

Submitting to his gentle tug, she plopped on the edge of the bed facing away from him.

"I'm a farmer Lydia. That's who I am. Beth wants to be a farm wife and start a family, so it makes sense."

She hugged her knees to her chest. The edges of the blanket cradled around her like a nest as she hung her head, attempting to veil the hurt.

Gabe sat up behind her, touching her arm. "I never stopped thinking about you. But I knew you were married. I couldn't mourn you forever. I had to move on with my life."

Lydia swallowed the lump in her throat. "You're right, Gabe," she said, touching his hand. "I'm married. I made my choice with vows to another man."

She lifted her chin and looked at him over her shoulder. "You've made a promise, too. I know you won't break it. I wouldn't expect you to."

His face filled with anguish.

She twisted toward him and pressed her fingertip to his lips. "Our lives have different directions, different commitments." Tears brimmed her eyes.

Gabe caressed the length of her arm with a gentle touch and pressed against her, kissing the back of her neck. "Stay with me now, for the short time we have left together."

His touch sparked the hunger for lovemaking. Leaning into him, she pressed her mouth to his with a tender touch, tasting the salty sweetness of his lips mixed with her tears. She rose from the bed. "I'll always love you, Gabe." She dressed and walked out of the trailer.

Chapter 26

Thursday Evening

Melissa paced around the living room of the farmhouse after Gabe had retired to bed for the evening. Reflections of the day's events at the funeral and the talk with Angela pushed aside any hope of sleep despite her exhaustion. Pouring a glass of bourbon with a splash of water, she sank into the comfort of the living room couch. Doc had settled onto the rug nearby and looked up at her. She raised the glass to her lips.

"Okay, Doc," she said returning his stare. "We are out of my usual herbal tea, so I had to find a substitute."

Doc lowered his head between his paws.

The aroma of the alcohol filled her nose. Tonight called for something much stronger than chamomile tea. The liquor heated her throat, and she leaned back, resting her head against the plush cushions.

The image of Angela's face formed behind Melissa's closed eyes. The woman had filled in some of the blanks from her account of Lydia's life. Did her mom really have love and concern for Melissa as Angela claimed, or did she run away out of selfish desires as her father asserted? Melissa had reason to trust her father, but no reason to trust Angela.

The trauma of her parent's argument the day her mother left replayed again in bursts of partial flashes. Her father's clenched fists, eyes burning with fire. Angry voices. Her mother's tears saturating a face twisted in despair. Melissa couldn't remember the context of the argument, alt-hough she had tried many times. The only words she couldn't forget rumbled like thunder. Your mother is leaving us, Melissa.

She took a long draw of the bourbon, savoring its heady effect. Her mother's spirit hovered everywhere here. The image of the corpse in the casket haunted Melissa. Why did she have a feeling of something else she needed to know?

Her eyes fixed on the framed photos on the bookshelf. Pictures of her mother with Gabe posing in a wooded area overlooking a river. A much younger Gabe holding a blue ribbon at a dairy cattle show. Remnants from the past Melissa had never known. A wave of sadness touched her as she accepted the glaring absence of any recent mother-and-daughter pictures.

The lack of photographs did not prevent her childhood memories from emerging. Happy times had once been shared between Melissa and her mom. She must have been eight or nine years old when Lydia showed her how to draw a clown with circles and triangles. After graduating from crayons to colored pencils, the mastery of rendition, although crude, brought her a sense of accomplishment.

Her mother showed her the nuance of color observed in art and nature when they visited the art museum or took walks together in the park. Flea markets provided a shopping pastime they shared. Although Melissa preferred the mall as a teenager, she marveled at her mom's ability to re-purpose discarded objects that others considered a lost cause. An odd piece of cloth could be fashioned into a craft project. A tattered postcard of a long-forgotten byway could be pasted into a collage.

Melissa gulped down the remainder of the drink. Rain drummed against the roof in a steady rhythm and the combination of its resonance, and the booze relaxed her until the lure of sleep beckoned.

Reaching over to turn off the table lamp and head for her

room, she noticed an amber glow in the direction of the stairway. The source of the illumination came from somewhere upstairs. She rose from the couch and walked toward the faint light. Did it come from the studio? Gabe always kept the studio door closed. It seemed unlikely he would have opened the door and left a light on.

Melissa stood at the bottom of the stairway with her hand on the mahogany rail and looked upward. The light glowed warm and diffused yet brightened the second-story walkway with exaggerated intensity. Her previous rumination faded, replaced with curiosity. She ascended the stair-way and followed the light source to the opened doorway of the studio. Doc sauntered close behind and sat at the door's threshold. His ears twitched forward.

A single lightbulb radiated from a floor lamp positioned beside the desk. Strange she had not noticed the lamp before. She paused to study it. Moving closer, she recognized the familiar scrollwork on the bronze base and the linear grapevine pattern that wound upward along the tubular column. She had been around ten years old or so when she and her mother found this lamp at a vintage store on one of their shopping excursions. A wonderful example of the Art Nouveau period, her mother had explained. Although Melissa didn't understand what that meant at the time, she ad-mired the way it looked like a tall flower. The lamp resided in the basement studio at the family home.

She stood a moment by the lamp before reaching for the off switch. Something caught her eye and her hand dropped. Beside the lamp, a hefty size art book lay on the desk opened to display a chapter entitled Women Artists of the Impressionism Movement. A full-page color image of a painting by Mary Cassatt portrayed a figure of a woman in a long, striped dress washing her young child's feet in a basin of water. Melissa recalled seeing this image in a book from her high school art class and later, the actual painting at an exhibit in San Francisco. The artwork theme struck her as a tender moment between mother and child.

Nestled behind the illustration, a bookmark protruded from the top. She turned the page. In the book's middle rested, not a bookmark, but a light blue envelope. The same stationery as the other two letters Melissa had read. Holding her breath, she removed the envelope and sat on the desk chair examining the front. Melissa's name appeared on the mail face but had no address, stamp, or postmark like the previous letters.

***

August 2010

Dear Melissa,

I write this letter because I'm afraid we may never talk again even though I desperately want to connect with you. I need to ask your forgiveness for a secret I've kept from everyone for decades. Only Gabe knows and now so will you. I wanted to tell you in person at the wedding two years ago and many, many times before that. How I've hoped and prayed I could reconcile with you before it's too late, to tell you everything you need to know. But I never knew how to do that or when the time was right. I've been a coward, so it is with all my strength that I gather my courage knowing you may fully and completely reject me forever.

This letter is my confession to you.

I believe Gabe is your real father, not Robert.

Melissa stopped reading and rubbed her forehead. The words echoed in her head–Gabe is your real father. She pictured her mother saying this in a remorseful tone. Perhaps with a sigh of relief from releasing a long-held silence. Or maybe voicing her delusional wish.

Even though Gabe had already softened the blow of the idea, it didn't make it any more palatable. The letter had been written eight years ago. What if she had known then about her mother's secret? Why wasn't this letter mailed like the others? If it had been sent, would she have opened it, or would it have shared the same fate as the others?

> I've kept this hidden all these years because I really didn't know for sure that you weren't Robert's child. Robert's name, of course, is on your birth certificate as the father. We were married after all, and there was never a question about parentage or being a normal family. We both wanted you very much and were so happy when you were born. When I saw you for the first time, my beautiful newborn daughter with your blue eyes, ivory skin, and the mass of black hair, my heart knew your real father was Gabe. I grew even more convinced as you got older. Sometimes you would have a look or mannerism that reminded me of him. Your features were so much alike.
> Please don't blame Gabe for this. I never told him until we started dating long after the divorce from Robert. When you were conceived, I was married, and he was engaged. I have lived my life with the guilt and shame of my actions and decisions, but never the outcome of bringing you into the world. If I had just taken a different direction, maybe our lives would have been hap-pier.
> I know you may hate me forever. I offer no excuses for what I've done. I only want you to know the truth. To know I love you.
> - Mom.

Melissa sank back in the chair, dropping her hands to her sides, still grasping the letter. Its contrite tone read so desperate. Pitiful, really. The regret and guilt must have tormented her mother. Did her father suspect this? If he did, he never indicated she was anything but his own flesh and blood.

She returned the letter to the desk and rose to shut the light off. Doc had not moved from the doorway. His wide eyes locked transfixed on the lamp, his tail swung back and forth. Melissa turned off the light and stepped out of the room, closing the door. "Let's go, Doc," she said, waiting for him to follow. He stood momentarily at her command, but instead of heeding her, he circled once, plopped down, and huddled outside the closed door.

Chapter 27

Friday Morning

Melissa sat at the kitchen table just as the sun peeked above the cliffs and filled the valley with light. She scrolled through her phone to check messages. The unfinished text reply to Jeremy still lingered on the screen from yesterday afternoon. She had forgotten about it. A phone call may be the best response instead of trying to write something back. Maybe a date for coffee would be interesting. She punched in his phone number.

A woman answered on the second ring. Her voice sounded perky and youthful.

Melissa checked the digits on the screen.

"Uh, I may have the wrong number. I'm looking for Jeremy. Is he there?"

"He's asleep," the woman said. "We were out kind of late last night."

Her giggle made Melissa flush with embarrassment for intruding into a situation she had not expected.

"Can I tell him who's calling?"

Words stuck in her throat as she formulated a response.

"Hello? Are you still there? Do you want to leave a message?"

"No, no message. Sorry to bother you." Melissa hung up.

She stroked her cheek with agitation, doubting her judgment lately. Jeremy seemed so genuine. How could she be so gullible and fall for his flirtation? He's attractive and friendly. Did she think he sat alone at home thinking about her? Of course, he's probably in a relationship. Maybe even married. What a player.

Gabe ambled into the kitchen, rubbing sleep from his eyes. "Good morning. I slept later than usual." He stared at her. "You look worried. What's up?"

She blew out a breath to chase away the phone call. "Nothing. I'm fine." She forced a smile, hoping to purge yet another disappointment on the dating front.

"How did you sleep?" he asked, pouring a cup of coffee.

Melissa shook her head, redirecting her thoughts. "Well, I had a hard time getting to sleep last night. So, I had a glass of your bourbon."

"Did it help?"

She shrugged. "I found something interesting, though."

"What?' Gabe asked, stirring cream into his cup.

"I found another letter from Mom," Melissa said.

"Really? What did it say?"

"Just how sorry she was, a confession that you know, uh ... she thought you were my father and not to blame you since she didn't tell you." Shifting in her chair, she propped her elbow on the table, tapped her cheek, and watched his face for a reaction.

He raised his eyebrows and sounded surprised. "Oh? Where did you find it?"

"In the studio, inside an art book. It was addressed to me but never mailed. Did you know about it?"

"She wrote a lot of letters, then threw them away. I think she gave up on the hope of hearing from you. I don't recall more than the two letters I showed you."

"I thought maybe you found it and put it into the book. I probably wouldn't have discovered it if you hadn't left the door open and light on."

"What do you mean?" Gabe looked over his coffee cup, his brow furrowed.

Melissa's face scrunched. "Well, maybe she put it there and I just didn't notice when I was in the studio earlier."

"Could be. But what do you mean the door was open and the light was on?"

"Didn't you leave the light on last night?" Melissa cocked her head toward him.

"No, I haven't been in the studio since we were in there together. I always keep the door closed."

She frowned, picturing the scene. "The door was open and the floor lamp we had when I was a kid was there. It was lit up. The book was open to where I found the letter."

Gabe rubbed his jaw. "Melissa, I didn't open the door and there has never been a floor lamp there."

"You're joking, right? You didn't set this whole thing up?" Melissa sat up straight in the chair.

Gabe shook his head. "No."

They shared confused expressions before Gabe spoke.

"It was late. Maybe it was the alcohol. You probably dreamed it."

Her breath quickened, annoyed at the turn of the conversation. Irritation from the phone call combined with Gabe insinuating she made it up, grated on her.

"Well, I know what I saw."

She launched away from the table and stormed upstairs to the studio. Gabe followed.

The art book lay opened to the page of the Cassatt painting exactly as she remembered with the letter on the desk. Grasping the letter, she waved it in the air and then slapped it down on the desk. "See, just like I told you."

Gabe stood by the doorway and watched her with a blank look.

Her eyes darted back and forth, scanning the room for the familiar lamp. Only a small desk light resided where the floor lamp had appeared. She marched to the closet and began to search inside.

Gabe walked over to the desk, grasping the base of the small desk lamp, and turned it over to examine it. "Probably has an electrical short that causes it to go on unexpectedly." He squinted at the lamp, jiggling the switch.

"No, Gabe, that wasn't the light I saw." Her voice boomed inside the closet. She pushed aside a fray of musty fabric and rummaged through corners piled with stacked boxes.

"Doc saw it too." Speaking the words, she realized she had just offered a dog as a witness.

Finding only stacks of used art supplies, shoes, and a paint-blotched smock, she paused her burrowing and took a breath. Her argument sounded crazy. Perhaps this was the beginning of a nervous breakdown. She turned toward Gabe. He sat bent forward in the chair by the desk, the letter quivering in his hand as he read it.

Trying to make sense of the situation only intensified her frustration. "Is this some kind of joke?" She plunked her hands on her hips and glared at him.

Gabe looked up at her, his face haggard. "Melissa, I'm sure there is some logical explanation."

She threw her arms up and pressed her palms against either side of her head, fingertips digging into her scalp. "I feel like I'm going crazy. I can't take any more surprises or revelations ... from anyone."

Gabe set the letter back on the desk and opened his mouth as if to say something. Without waiting for a response, she rushed past him. "I'm leaving. I'm getting out of here now." She whisked through the studio door and stomped down the stairs.

***

"What are you doing?" Gabe asked, standing in the doorway of her room watching Melissa throw her suitcase onto the bed.

Try as she might to control her anger, it spewed out unrestricted. "I'm packing ... I'll get an earlier flight home. I can't take all the emotional strain anymore. This has all been a waste of time. I feel her ghost everywhere and now I'm imagining things."

"Whoa, slow down, Melissa," Gabe said holding the palms of his hands up. "I'm sure we can talk about this. Lydia just wanted you to understand ..."

"No, Gabe," she interrupted. "Do not tell me what a wonderful person my mother was. People say that but they don't know the depth of her deceit. Mom left me and had a lesbian affair, for Christ's sake! She even lied about something as important as who my father is ... oh, yes, she wasn't completely sure about that. Kind of shows a pattern of infidelity, doesn't it?"

Pulling drawers out, she grabbed shirts crumpled in a heap and jettisoned them into the open suitcase.

"Mom went around trying to satisfy her own needs – only thought about herself. My dad was right. She was a self-centered bitch!"

Gabe frowned and walked into the room. His voice turned serious. "Maybe you need to look at who is self-centered, Melissa."

Her body stiffened as she looked up from her chore, eyes wide in surprise at the tone of voice she had not heard before.

He leaned in closer to her. "You are so focused on yourself you can't see what she had to go through. She stayed in an emotionally abusive marriage so you could be raised by both parents. Robert provided security. And from what Lydia told me, he adored you–treated you differently than he did her."

She frowned and thrust her chin forward. "You don't leave your family just because somebody says some mean stuff once in a while." She punched down a crumpled blouse with her fist into the corner of the suitcase. "Dad was never violent toward her. If he was, I would have seen it. I would have seen bruises or black eyes."

"No, he didn't physically hurt her," Gabe said. "But the constant belittlement and his insistence on control of her took its toll.

Her self-esteem became so shredded, she doubted her decisions. She traded her happiness for what she thought was best for you." Melissa stopped packing and planted her hands on her hips. "Oh, puh-leez, Gabe, that's such a feeble excuse. Mom stayed for me? So, it's my fault she didn't have a happy life?"

"No," Gabe breathed an exasperated sigh. "That's not what I meant. She just did what she thought was right. She was scared of her ability to have a life away from him, to be able to support herself and you. Robert could provide a much richer life than she could ever do by herself. I mean, think about it. Could she have afforded your education? She didn't want you to repeat her mistakes because college wasn't an option. No, Melissa, she chose to do what she did because she was thinking of your welfare."

Melissa turned away from him, squeezed her eyes shut, and rubbed her temples. Her head throbbed.

"Look, Melissa, I'm no relationship expert, but it seems to me you had a pretty good life, lived in a nice neighborhood, went to good schools, and got a college education." His voice became elevated and tense. "Did you have to deal with any real hardship?"

Melissa pivoted toward him and scowled, "How do you know what my life was like, Gabe? You weren't there, remember?"

He hesitated. "No, I wasn't there, but I would have asked her to marry me before you were born if she would have had me." His voice lowered. "If I had known that she was pregnant with you, I'd have taken different actions. My life would have been different too. I didn't want to bust up her marriage and she didn't want me to break my engagement. She made decisions based on her only options. Maybe Lydia didn't do everything right, but who does? We're all human. We all must accept that we make mistakes and learn to forgive. You had the chance to set the situation right when she reached out to you, and you chose to ignore her invitations."

"Well, it's a little too late for all that now, isn't it, Gabe?" She stood straight and crossed her arms against her chest.

He shook his head. "So where should we point fingers? You were the one so stuck on the fact she left. You couldn't forgive her even when she tried to reach out to you. What was your role in the estrangement? Did you think it was all up to her to repair the relationship? She tried the best way she knew how. Take some responsibility for your own actions, Melissa."

Her throat tightened and she huffed out an exaggerated breath, slamming the lid of the suitcase. "Why did I ever come here? Just to find more deception? More dishonesty than I imagined? To confirm all her lies?"

"Melissa," his voice breathed low and stern. "It's not lies you've found. It's truth."

She inhaled a sob and dropped onto the chair next to the bed, cradling her head in her hands.

Gabe's voice softened. "I think the reason you came here is that deep inside, you needed to find the truth, to forgive and be forgiven. It was too late to do that in her lifetime. But maybe somehow you can resolve this by finding it in your heart to forgive yourself." Gabe rested his hand on the back of her chair. "Accept you are only human too and learn from past mistakes. You are the only one with the power to make yourself happy. No one can give that to you. When you forever blame someone else, you'll never find happiness."

Her face burned and she jumped up in a defiant stance. "I'm done, Gabe! You can lecture me, but you can't stop me from leaving. I'll find a cab to the airport."

He moved toward the door, looking back over his shoulder with a hint of a smile.

"Why are you looking at me like that?" she growled.

"Well, you're not in the city. There are no cabs around here." Gabe shook his head in resignation. "I'll take you to the airport if that's what you want, but I hope you reconsider and not leave like this."

She brought a stiff arm up, fingers spread, prepared to push him out but he had already retreated into the hall right before she slammed the bedroom door. Punching her fists in the air, she swallowed a scream.

Chapter 28

Lydia and Robert 1977

Lydia parked the car in the driveway of the rented bungalow where she and Robert lived. The late afternoon sun filtered through the branches of the Ash tree in the front yard, but its meager shade did nothing to cool the day's heat. She retrieved the house keys from her purse and ambled to the front door. Humidity clung to her like tears leaching from every pore of her body. She wiped her cheek with the back of her hand in a vain effort to sweep the flood of emotion away. The mix of joy and happiness yesterday with Gabe stood in sharp contrast to the heartbreak and loneliness parting from him today.

Unlocking the door, she entered the dim entryway, no larger than a closet. Stepping into the adjacent living room, she reached to shut the front door, but it started to close by itself.

A shadowed figure burst from behind it and lurched toward her. Screaming, her arms flew upwards in a protective instinct. She tumbled through the air. When her backside met the living room floor with a thud, a shock pulsed through her hip. Pain radiated across her elbow.

"God damn it! You scared the shit out of me."

Robert towered in front of her like a granite statue. Arms hung at his sides and his dark eyes shot a searing look.

Her entire body trembled as she gasped for air.

"Did you miss me?" he asked in a sinister voice.

Lydia raised herself with one hand and pressed the other against her chest to calm her pounding heart. She took a deep breath. "That's not funny, Robert. Why would you do that?"

His face remained stony except for a slight sneer. Narrowed eyes scanned her up and down. "Where have you been?" The question held a menacing tone.

Her heels dug into the floor, and she pushed away from him, locking onto his expression to gauge his next move. He scrutinized her with a fixed glare.

She gathered her purse along with her senses. Spilled contents sprawled across the floor, and she scooped up the keys that had ejected from her grasp. Trembling, she shoved lipstick, tissues, and a pen back into the purse and zipped it closed. Rising from the awkward position, she brushed her hair back out of her face and took a deep breath to steady her voice. "I finished my volunteer work and since it was the last day of the fair everyone needed to help clean up, so I stayed a little longer, you know, to help."

Robert's targeted frown appeared to calculate the honesty of her explanation.

She managed a nervous smile. "I wasn't expecting you until tomorrow. How was your trip?" Maybe her friendly tone would diffuse the likelihood of an impending argument.

He turned and walked toward the couch without speaking. She had learned to recognize his brooding as a signal that he needed to appease or suffer the consequences. At times his moodiness became unbearable. The solution usually entailed either staying out of his way or offering something he'd like.

"Do you want anything to eat?" she asked, making her way to the kitchen.

"Bring me a beer," he answered, switching on the television, and settling onto the couch. She grabbed a can from the fridge and placed it on the coffee table next to him.

He glanced at the beer but made no comment.

"I can make a meatloaf and mashed potatoes for dinner." Her voice sounded weak.

He took a swig of the brew, not moving his eyes from the TV. "Don't bother."

She took this as a sign that maybe he was offering her a break from cooking tonight.

Instead, he said, "Your meatloaf tastes like shit. I'll find something for myself."

Her mouth tightened as she choked back the despair and frustration. "I'm sure you're tired from your trip." She turned and crept away, retreating into the bedroom for the rest of the evening.

***

That night Lydia lay in bed alone, staring upward, trying to quell the misery racing through her mind. Deep emptiness gnawed her as she thought about Gabe. But she had told him she couldn't leave her husband. Vows of faithfulness needed abidance.

Robert had fallen asleep on the couch, and she didn't want to wake him. Or guess how to soothe his foul mood.

Evening shadows danced across the room. Moonlight created silhouettes from tree branches that snaked across the ceiling like flickering bars of a prison cell. Guilt over her infidelity filled her with shame. Perhaps in some way, she deserved Robert's harsh and moody episodes. With effort, things would get better. Robert needed her. It wasn't only the marriage, but her aging mother needed her too. Ruth lived alone in a tiny apartment and was getting up in years.

Now was not the time for life-altering changes. Disrupting daily routines seemed to aggravate Robert, so she must be careful and avoid deviating too much from his schedule. Her mother's words echoed in her thoughts too. Reasons to be grateful for her hard-working husband.

It would be awful to be alone, impossible to support herself and her mother. Robert had told her this several times. He pointed out that without him, she would not only be alone, but too old for another man to want her. Any job she managed to get wouldn't provide enough income for the monthly grocery bill, much less all the other expenses of life.

She fell asleep with determination to be a good wife.

Light from the hallway poured into the bedroom when the door opened and startled her. Robert stood naked next to the bed, his shadow falling across her. "Wake up," he demanded as he pulled the covers away and crawled in beside her.

"What's the matter? What is it?" Lydia rubbed her eyes.

His hand slithered underneath her nightgown and grabbed her breast with an abruptness that made her gasp.

"Robert, I'm sleeping. What time is it?" Lydia pushed his hand away, but he clenched her arm. In one swift movement, he flipped her over to her belly. His other hand moved with urgency to crumple her nightgown up around her waist and pull her hips up against his groin.

"Wait, Robert, stop! You're hurting me."

Her plea went unheeded as he thrust the weight of his body hard between her legs. The pain made her cringe.

"I know you want this. You've been teasing me ever since I got home." His pounding against her quickened. Her cries weren't the kind summoned from pleasure but from humiliation. The only desire she felt was to escape into the darkness. To disappear.

When he finished, he slapped her butt in the final insult and dropped beside her. Within minutes he started to snore.

***

The next morning, she awoke and sauntered to the kitchen for her morning coffee. Robert sat at the dining room table, chewing toast and reading the newspaper.

"Good, you're finally awake." He put his newspaper down. "Sit," he said, pointing to the dining room chair, as he strode to the coffee pot on the counter.

Lydia sat down but waited to speak or offer any comments before she gauged the reason for his light mood. A stark contrast from the previous day. He placed a steaming cup of coffee in front of her and sat across the table.

"I have great news." He thrust out his chin and let the statement linger with a dramatic pause. "Remember I told you over the phone about a surprise?

Lydia nodded, recalling his comment, and took a sip of coffee, waiting for his big reveal.

He straightened his shoulders and beamed a toothy grin. "The boss has been impressed with me and I've been promoted to Regional Construction Materials Manager. That means a big pay increase and a nice, cushy office at headquarters."

"That's wonderful, Robert." She smiled with genuine surprise. "I know you've been hoping for this promotion. You deserve it."

"I'm a big asset to the company," he said with a wave of his hand. "And they know it. I make a ton of money for them because I understand the importance of profit. It's simple, really. I charge the customer the premium price but get the cheaper materials."

"Really? Isn't that unethical?" Lydia asked in a timid voice.

He snorted out a huff and snapped back with a pointed finger. "You don't know anything about business, Lydia. This is how things are done. Everybody does it. The stupid customer doesn't even notice, so what's the harm?" His posture relaxed. "Just stick to your household role. It'll make your life simpler."

She looked away, tipping the coffee cup to her lips to hide her frown.

"Oh, honey, don't bother yourself with details," his voice turned buttery. "Wait, I have another surprise for you."

He jumped up from the table and hustled into the living room.

When he returned, he carried a small gold jewelry box. "You're going to love this," he said.

Lydia's face lit up with anticipation. "What is it?"

"Well, open it, darling, and find out."

She lifted the lid and found a folded piece of paper which she pushed aside, expecting something underneath that sparkled.

"Look, Lydia, the picture."

Taking the paper in hand, she unfolded it and stared at a magazine clipping. Curiosity displaced her immediate disappointment. "This is an artist's rendition of a house."

He nodded. "I've already got blueprints for it ordered." Robert leaned toward her with a puffed-up smile.

Her mouth dropped open. "A new house? Our house? I can't believe it."

"Now we can build that house you're always harping about," he said and leaned back in the chair.

A house of her own. Something she had always dreamed about. Perhaps her fears and misgivings about her marriage could reverse course with this news.

She studied the sketch of the two-story structure set in a landscape of leafy trees, a large picture window in front. "Does it have a solarium? A big kitchen?"

"Don't overreach, honey. I've got it all figured out. We have a budget, you know."

"Yes, of course. I can't wait to tell Mom." Lydia hoped this signaled an upturn in their relationship, a fresh start with a home they owned and built together.

Robert pushed his plate of partially eaten breakfast away and rose from the table. "I thought you'd be happy about that. Now I'm going to play some golf. Oh, yes, let's have dinner at 6:00 tonight. Get good steaks this time. The last ones you got were too gristled."

Chapter 29

Friday

After the argument with Gabe in the studio Thursday evening, Melissa sequestered herself in her room, alone with her disgruntled mood, nursing a bruised ego. Gabe had treated her like a child. Treatment she would not tolerate, especially from a man she barely knew and who didn't know her. The emotional strain of the last few days left her exhausted as if she had maneuvered through a battleground filled with landmines. Airline reservations could wait until later. All she wanted to do was sleep.

***

She awoke late Friday morning, after a restless night's sleep. Fatigue from the barrage of events caused her to lash out at Gabe, and she felt a bit sheepish about the argument. The idea of apologizing for her outburst crossed her mind. But maybe later. Her first goal aimed to make travel arrangements and depart as soon as possible.

When Gabe knocked on her door and asked if she wanted lunch, she dismissed him with a flat tone. "No thanks, I'll get something later."

Grabbing her iPhone, she opened the app for the airline. The Internet service displayed never-ending spinning circles. After several attempts, she tried calling the ticket center but fared no better. At first, her connection had been answered by a recording and put on hold. After several minutes, it disconnected. Determined, she tried again and again until she watched the mobile service bars dwindle to nothing. She threw the phone on the bed in frustration.

After wasting the entire morning and part of the afternoon mired in failure with rural technology, she concluded her choices would be to either give up the idea of an earlier departure or ask for Gabe's help. He could drive her into town to a cafe with wi-fi or somewhere other than this wilderness. But asking for a favor would require her to explain how she couldn't stand one more day of his high-and-mighty attitude toward her, all while spending his time and courtesy of helping her get home. A persistent throbbing pounded in the back of her head. Best to avoid Gabe for the time being or any conversation about their fight. Enduring one more day before her scheduled flight back to civilization would be inconvenient, but not impossible.

The sound of clanking dishes from the kitchen sounded like he probably had finished lunch. The back door closed, and his voice carried from outside. Likely talking to Doc. When his car rumbled past her window and out the driveway, she walked to the kitchen and peered outside in all directions. No sign of either Gabe or Doc.

She gobbled down a peanut butter sandwich and paced the kitchen. The house was quiet except for the mechanized rhythm of the dishwasher. Restlessness overtook her boredom, and she grabbed her jacket, slipping her feet into her mom's ridiculous boots. The thought occurred to her to leave a note about taking a stroll, but she decided against it. A short hike and fresh air would relieve her headache and stretch her legs. Donning her jacket, she headed outside.

After the first ten minutes of brisk walking through the grassy pasture that sprouted colorful wildflowers, her tension diminished. Afternoon sunshine warmed her face, and the air smelled of autumn leaves. Her headache began to subside.

About a half-mile from the house, just as the thought of returning entered her mind, she discovered a flattened layer of vegetation bordered by taller grass. A path appeared to wind up the tree-covered hillside. The beckoning woods intrigued her, and she found herself drawn into its shady comfort.

Climbing the meandering trail became a daunting task with its ascending slope. Breaths came faster and deeper as she navigated around the wet puddles that littered the path. Trail shoes would have provided better footing—the ones she preferred for trekking through the urban greenbelt of Golden Gate Park. Sticky mud clung to her boots and attracted scattered stones like a magnet that burrowed into the thin rubber soles. Tree roots protruding just above the bumpy dirt surface caused her to stumble but didn't dampen her progress. Curiosity invigorated her energy, and she ignored the minor discomfort. Any lingering anger and frustration fed into the physical challenge and empowered her.

After a while, she slowed her pace, raising her chin upward. A dense canopy of trees obscured the view of the late afternoon sky. Occasional flickering of sunlight momentarily shimmered across the path. Falling leaves from oaks and maples swayed downward in gentle slow motion. Any fatigue from the hike vanished when she stopped and inhaled the crisp scent of fresh air.

Murmurs of nature from the forest whispered a tranquil lull that calmed her anxiety. Creaking and rustling from the woodland punctuated by the sharp twill and chirp of hidden birds produced its own melody.

Thoughts of the unpleasant argument with Gabe sparked a touch of guilt for her overreaction. He must think she's a terrible person. The anguish and discontent plaguing her ever since she arrived finally had burst open and he became the receiver. The act of burying her mother simultaneously unearthed feelings once packed deep within her core. Painful memories she didn't want to confront. She disdained displays of over-the-top emotion, especially in herself. Much simpler to tuck it away and forget.

Why did so many relationships disappoint her? When someone became too close, whatever bond existed usually ended with a major disagreement. As soon as she trusted someone, that trust would be betrayed in one way or another.

Her failed marriage and other dating interests had a pattern. She initiated the breakups. Dr. Prescott had pinpointed something she had not thought about–the pattern of leaving. Maybe she sabotaged her happiness. Did she do the same with Gabe? Wreck a relationship before it barely began? The same with Jeremy–a too-good-to-be-true potential. A deep rush of loneliness drained through her. Destined to be alone. The thought pressed her to look where she didn't want to go. Gabe's terse words barged into her mind. You looked for lies but found truth instead.

She rested near the top of the hill to catch her breath, closing her eyes and inhaling the heady fragrance of damp earth and pine. The scent conjured the memory of her mother's freshly dug grave and the fact that she was gone forever.

"Why weren't you the mother I needed?" she said out loud. Her face pinched. "Why didn't you love me? I just wanted you to love me." She brushed the corner of her eye with her fingertips.

A hawk screeched overhead and brought her attention skyward to the canopy of twisting branches clutching their remaining leaves. The path ahead appeared blocked by the density of tree trunks and towering, large rocks. The trail's dead-end convinced her to head back.

She turned and noticed an area close by that tunneled through the woods where the brushy wall of forest parted. A sliver of deep blue sky peeked through a section small enough to have been unobserved at another angle but large enough to beg investigation. Venturing through the growth of conifers, her cautious footsteps tread upon the layered forest floor, cushioned with years of accumulated pine needles. She emerged to a scene that caused a swift intake of breath, not from the exertion, but the panorama.

The expanse of the vista below painted sweeping brushstrokes of far-flung hills appearing violet from their distance. Tops of pine trees formed a carpet of undulating textures with various shades of green. A winding, silver river sparkled and meandered through the lowland, transecting the rise of stony ridges.

Standing near the edge where the cliff dropped off, she drank in the enormous view that surrounded her. Spreading her arms wide, she felt like a bird soaring over the earth.

Brilliant autumn foliage dotted lush pastures infused with the colors of sienna and ochre. Yellow, crimson, and oranges splashed against a background of turquoise sky.

She situated herself on a flat rock, absorbing the sight. A lightness filled the spaces of anxiety and washed over her as she breathed in nature's display. Worries shrank to something small and insignificant. Her physical presence became a minute speck in the universe, invited by some unseen force of fate to exist in this appointed space for only a moment.

Earth and heaven competed for which flaunted the most beauty. The fiery rays of sunset reflected translucent pink off voluminous clouds that appeared in a rich dimension of highlights and shadows.

Time shifted and stretched, then stood still. Its fleeting passage evaded her as she became mesmerized by this mystical place. The quiet solitude summoned contemplation about the past few days. For the first time, it became clear what she needed to do.

***

Sundown burned away, replaced by darkening clouds. She turned to retrace her steps back down the hill, zipping her jacket from the sudden chill. Twilight had engulfed the forest. She scanned the area for the path. Muscles tensed as she searched for the lost direction. Stepping one way, and turning another, she picked her way downhill, looking for familiar landmarks. Trees and foliage appeared identical, like inside a hall of mirrors. The path, so defined what seemed like only moments ago, had disappeared, blanketed by creeping nightfall and erased by leaves that covered the ground. Filtered sunlight that soothed her uphill journey disappeared. Dense shadow, murky as a bay area fog, fell around her.

She reached into the pocket of her jacket for her phone to use the flashlight and GPS. "Damn it!" She swore out loud, cursing her foolishness for leaving it plugged into the charger at the house. In her haste to escape the claustrophobic house, she had forgotten to take it. A shiver ran through her, both from her rising apprehension and the ensuing temperature drop.

No longer a pleasing nature stroll, she hurried her pace and descended passed trees that previously exuded serenity but now transformed into threatening shapes. Shadows advanced with each gust of increasing wind. Large tree branches bent like bony fingers across the path. Her heart raced.

Without warning, the toe of her boot caught on something snaking across the rugged surface. The exposed tree root extended only a few inches above the ground, just enough to catch her quickening footsteps. Her body lurched, wrenching forward into a free fall. A cracking sound accompanied by a sharp pain in her ankle sent her tumbling. Her shoulder met the forest floor with a heavy thud. Wincing, she squeezed her eyes shut as she reached toward her foot. "Shit!" Her cry dissipated into the darkening forest.

She pushed herself up, tore off her boot, and rubbed her ankle. Her actions did little to ease the growing discomfort. Feeling the heat of the swollen area, she quickly pulled the boot back on before the swelling increased and she'd be left to hobble around in stocking feet.

Bits of damp detritus clung to her jacket, and she brushed away the sticky dirt that smeared the lightweight fabric.

"Oh, great, just wonderful. What else can go wrong?"

Breathing came in short bursts and her eyes watered. Sobs bellowed with a gusto rarely unleashed, allowed to blast forth. Salty tears burned her cheeks, and she wiped them away with her hand gritty from dirt.

A hoot of an unseen owl pierced the air. Its forlorn call turned her sobs into sniffles. The thought of wild animals switched her into defense mode. Raccoons and badgers probably hid nearby. Sherry had mentioned sightings of bobcats, too. She tucked the worry away. More immediate things needed her full attention.

Pain radiated from her ankle and shot up her leg when she tried to stand. Attempting to balance on one foot failed, and her hip took the brunt of her fall. Blinded by the darkness, she patted the ground around her, fumbling to find anything to help her up. Something crawled across her wrist, and she grimaced in disgust, jerking her hand back.

A cold wind blew around her and she pulled the drawstring of the jacket hood tighter. Low rumbling of thunder preceded a scent of mustiness. Leaves quivered, catching large, wet drops splatting onto the outstretched foliage like a leaky umbrella. The rain that began as a gentle patter, no longer held at bay by the forest canopy, infiltrated through the woods. Raindrops fell with a fierceness, stinging her face and hands. Craving water, she opened her mouth and extended her tongue. The drops only teased her dry throat.

By the time the second thunderbolt rumbled, she had discovered a long stick. The weight of it felt sturdy. She thrust the uninjured foot forward. Using the stick and her good leg, she struggled to stand. Teetering with an unsteady gait, she inched along, treading the ground like a toddler learning to walk. The dull ache throbbing in her shoulder paled in comparison to each painful step. Muddy ground became slick as the rain formed sludge.

Trudging forward, her feet wobbled and slid out from under her. Flailing about with wild flapping gestures, she thudded onto her backside and toppled down a slope, bouncing out of control over the rocky surface. Sharp twigs poked her as she bumped and rolled over the ground with increasing velocity. Her rapid descent met an abrupt stop, crashing into something hard and solid. The world spun in a watery eddy of swirling black ink, sweeping her along rising and falling waves with no sense of physical space. The desire to sleep came over her. Sleep wrapped in darkness. Submission to the feeling of dissolving into the earth, lulled by a fading rhythm of raindrops, then no sound at all.

Chapter 30

Friday Evening

A buzzing sound grew inside Melissa's head. Her eyes popped open, and she found herself in the familiar space of her childhood bedroom. Dim yellow light glowed from the floor lamp. The ragged stuffed monkey Grandma knitted for her stared back from its place on the shelf in the corner of the room. Discolored yarn frayed around the edges of its soft frame from years of numerous hugs. Pencil drawings of clowns shared wall space with posters of musicians sprouting frenzied hair and painted eyes. Her senior prom dress hung like a specter inside the closet. She sat up in her twin bed. Rising voices from her parents came from the living room downstairs. Low tones heightened as the bedroom door opened by itself to reveal a frightening scene. Fear coursed through her as she crept to the second-story hallway and peered down to the living room. The wailing intensity of her parent's argument escalated. She watched, curled into a ball, hidden behind the loft's railing. They stood facing each other. Her mother's teary face compressed into something wild and unrecognizable. Her father's body pitched toward her. His arms steeled at his side with clenched fists.

Melissa couldn't believe the brutal words hurtled between them.

"I don't love you anymore, Robert! I'm leaving you and taking Melissa with me."

Robert rasped with a voice like gravel. "Go ahead and leave. But if you try to take Melissa, I guarantee I'll fight you. You'll never see her again. We'll move so far away you won't be able to find her. Leave now if you want but without her."

"You can't do that. She's my daughter!"

"I can and I will. You have nothing. No resources, no money. Christ, you can't even hold down a job. I'll close all the bank accounts. I have all the power."

"Robert, please, don't do this!" Her eyes widened, lips pulled up, revealing her teeth.

"You're a two-timing bitch! I know about your infidelity."

Lydia moved backward. Her mouth dropped open.

"How could you possibly know that?"

Silenced knifed the deadened air between them and neither spoke.

"I didn't know for sure until just now."

"Robert, I admit it was wrong, but it was only once. I never saw him again. Please don't punish our daughter for my actions. She needs me!" Her angry expression turned pleading.

His finger jabbed inches from her face. "You admit you two-timed me with a man! Now you're leaving me for a woman!"

"Robert, it's not like that. Angela has nothing to do with…"

He interrupted her with a voice dripping with venom. "Go live with your lesbian lover then! How does that look for your morality? Go on … leave. But Melissa stays here with me."

The scene went black as if Melissa had been sucked into a vacant chasm. No sound. She floated in a weightlessness, drifting in a cold void.

Hushed murmurs of a multitude of indistinct voices grew louder, unified and reverberating in echoes, only to be squelched when a single familiar voice emerged.

"Melissa, wake up."

She shuddered and opened her eyes. "Mom?"

The ephemeral sound of her mother's whisper faded away.

Blinking and groggy, Melissa dug her elbow into the stew of wet earth, propping herself halfway up. Her eyes darted around expecting to see a ghost. Only tree trunks and stubbles of ragged grass surrounded her. She ran her hands along the large stone pressing into her side.

"Is anyone out there?" A flutter of wings and caws from startled birds cracked the silence.

Her arm surrendered the attempt to hold steady and she dropped onto her back, staring up at the woodland's dark, leafy blanket. The vision of her parents hate-infused words had flooded back, awakening memories long repressed somewhere deep inside, sharpened to a razor-like certainty.

Physical awareness slapped her thoughts away as pain screamed for her attention. Cold leached beneath her skin, and her shivering body fought for warmth. Throbbing pain from her ankle and the rock jabbing her side felt like she had been hit by a heavyweight boxer.

Gabe would have no idea where to find her. He may have surmised she had left town like she had threatened to do. Images flashed behind her tightly squeezed eyes, envisioning the search party finding her sometime tomorrow, twisted and stiff, no longer breathing. Covered by a cragged mudslide. Found only by her wretched hand extended out from a quagmire of frost-laden mud. Poor girl, they would say, died only days after her mother's passing.

***

A coughing fit from an inhaled water droplet convulsed her upward, and she hung her head between shaky knees. A spasm from her ankle jolted along her leg and met the ache in her side.

The rain had stopped but left a lingering scent of wet earth and vegetation. Her shivering quieted. Despite her drenched jacket, the chill diminished into soggy stickiness. She rubbed her forehead to focus her disoriented thoughts. "It's time to go back to the house now," she whispered, her words dripped out. "I must tell Gabe ... I have to tell him something." She wiped her cheek with a mud-caked hand and tasted the watery grit that trickled to her lips.

Raising her head, she peered into the night. A rustling in the distance brought her awareness rushing back. Fear replaced grogginess and despite her rapid heartbeat, she held her breath. Something lurked nearby. The shape of some kind of animal paced closer. Seeking a weapon, she groped the ground and curled her fingers around a rock, straining her vision to assess her target. The dark figure looked to be the size and shape of a bobcat. She tightened her grip on the stone while the animal inched forward. Her arm tensed ready to hurl the rock with whatever strength she had left.

"Go away!" she choked out a weak cry.

A sharp bark pierced the air. Her clenched hand opened.

"Doc!" She cried out a sigh of relief. The dog materialized like an apparition from the shadows just as moonlight peeked from behind a cloud. Eyes glowed red like glistening marbles. His usual lumbering stride smoothed into a gliding gait and the rhythm of his tail swung like a hypnotic pendulum. Reaching out to meet him, she wrapped her arms around his neck and buried her face in his soft, furry shoulder. Expecting the odor of a wet dog, she instead inhaled the smell of flowers.

His appearance brought the hum of an engine, droning in the distance.

"Melissa." A faint call from far away drifted in the air, like in a dream.

"I'm here, Gabe!" The effort of shouting with intensity enough to be heard rocketed another surge of pain up her side. She pulled back from Doc, instinctively squeezing her eyes shut, and wrapped her hand around her ribs. When she looked up a moment later, he had disappeared.

"No, Doc, come back," she whimpered, thrusting her arms out into the stillness of the motionless forest.

Breathless, she waited for any kind of response, but the woods held only silence. No engine noise, no barking. Straining to listen for any sound, it frightened her to think she imagined it. Holding her side, she attempted another shout, but her parched mouth allowed only a feeble squeak.

Dizzy and weak, she collapsed back into the mud, looking skyward, resigned to whatever fate cared to do with her. Closing her eyes, a flickering image in shades of gray like a vintage film played. She watched her mother, surrounded by dust-covered family albums, turn toward her. A spotlight narrowed on her face. Lydia lifted her overly large eyes, out of proportion to her diminutive skull. Pale skin glowed luminous like a full moon in the night sky. Tender words breathed from her parted lips.

"You have the power within you, Melissa. You decide." After a moment, the vision abruptly shattered into a million sparkling fragments.

Melissa's eyes fluttered open as she drew in a quick breath. The moon shone through the branches, not quite full but unusually large. Pallid light cast wan shadows through the trees. Enough illumination to gauge her surroundings.

She gritted her teeth and rolled to her stomach with a groan. Ignoring her throbbing ankle, a new and surprising wave of determination bolstered her. Muscles infused with energy fueled only by willpower. With a deep breath, she grunted out loud, "I'm getting the hell outta here!"

Throwing her right arm out, she plunged her hand into the damp earth, fingernails boring in deep, creating a handhold. With the opposite leg, she bent her knee and burrowed her uninjured foot into the ground, pushing, heaving her body upward, crawling a few inches with each repeated exertion. With hands, knees, and elbows she pressed forward and up, climbing to a destination she couldn't plot or map. Driving ahead, inch by inch, minute by minute. She stretched, heaved, and pushed. Finally reaching level ground, exhausted, she stopped to catch her breath. With her last bit of strength, she raised to a sitting position, grimacing with the effort.

The sound of Gabe's shout cracked the silence, more distinct than before. "Melissa, can you hear me?"

His voice boomed out. He had to be close. The underbrush in front of her rustled with movement. Grass parted and Doc's head appeared, bobbing up and down as he lumbered toward her. A scattered beam from a flashlight followed behind him, swinging side to side.

She waved her arm in an exaggerated movement. "I'm here, Gabe. I slid down a hill."

Doc circled her, barking in loud, short bursts.

A light shone in her eyes. Shielding her face with an open palm, she heard footsteps crunching through the brush coming toward her.

"I see you!" he shouted.

Within a minute, he appeared by her side and crouched down, brushing her hair from her face. "Are you alright? Are you hurt?" Gabe's voice rasped with urgency.

"I think I broke my right ankle. Everything hurts." Tears of pain mixed with relief flooded her eyes and poured down her cheeks. "I'm really thirsty, too."

Gabe reached into a backpack he carried and brought out a water bottle, shoving it into her hand. "Here, drink this."

She grabbed it and gulped it down. Water had never tasted so good.

He ran his hand along her boot. "This one?"

"Ouch!" Melissa choked.

"Sorry. Can you stand up?"

"Yes, if you help me."

He took the water bottle and put it back into the pack. "Are you ready?"

She nodded.

His sturdy embrace raised her as she stood on one leg.

"We have to walk some, so lean on me. I left the ATV at the top of the hill since it can't get through the woods this far. I was really worried. Been searching for over an hour and ready to call the sheriff."

"I'm sorry Gabe, I got lost. I'm just really, really happy to see you" Tears fell unfettered as she wrapped her arm around his midsection.

"You're okay now," Gabe said as he steadied her. "Let's get you back home."

Chapter 31

Late Friday Evening

After a hot bath, Melissa sprawled on the couch, wrapped in her mother's terrycloth robe. Her ankle lay propped on top of a pillow.

Gabe appeared from the kitchen carrying a tray and placed it on her lap. Steam rose from the bowl, carrying the savory aroma of soup. A tumbler of water, three tablets of ibuprofen, and another shorter glass partially filled with whiskey accompanied the meal.

Melissa eagerly spooned in a mouthful of soup. "Oh, My God, this is Mom's ham and bean soup, isn't it?" She savored the flavor, licking her lips.

"Yup. I thawed out one of the serving sizes she had made a while ago."

"I remember this," Melissa said between bites. "Mom made it when I was a kid. She never wrote down a recipe. I didn't pay attention to how she cooked it."

Gabe lowered his head. An awkward silence fell between them as she ate, heavy with the predicted absence of past comforts. She finished the last drop of soup.

After a moment, he looked at her. "You sprained your ankle pretty good, but it's not broken, as far as I can tell. Keep it elevated and that ice pack on it." He pointed to her foot. "The athletic tape should keep the swelling down."

Raising her leg for a closer examination of Gabe's handiwork shot an immediate protest through her bruised ribs.

Gabe shifted in his chair and eyed her carefully. "You were only about a mile from the house and would have eventually made it back here without my help."

"Oh yes, I wasn't too worried about it." She swallowed a sip of the whiskey-water mix along with the bravado remark.

"But I'm sure glad you were there," she added. "Sorry for all the drama I caused."

He waved a dismissive hand. "If you're not feeling better by the morning, I'll take you into town to the hospital to get an X-ray."

"No, no." She shook her head. "I've been enough trouble. I'm fine. Feeling better already." She winced with a smile as she raised her glass to take another deep draw of the liquor.

"That may make it feel better, but you need to rehydrate. I'll be right back." Gabe retrieved the empty tray and plodded to the kitchen.

She leaned back and closed her eyes. Deciphering the events that happened in the woods challenged her sense of reality. Sharing the whole experience with him could wait until she sorted it out for herself. Would he believe her? The resurfaced memory of her parent's argument was so clearly recalled. The vision and voice of her mother loomed most baffling. The encounter defied logic, yet felt as real as the stones and earth that had surrounded her.

Gabe returned with another glass of ice water and placed it on the table beside her. He dropped into the chair across from her.

She looked at the water but held on to the bourbon. "Thanks, Gabe. I mean, thank you for everything you've done, for your help. I was lucky you found me."

"When I got back from the grocery store, I looked around the house for you. Then tried the barn. Foreman hadn't seen you."

"So, how did you know where to search?"

Gabe smiled. "I stood in the yard scratching my head." He

motioned to Doc lying on the floor. "I noticed him looking out toward the field. It gave me an idea of where to look. Lydia and Doc used to walk that path together."

Melissa cast her gaze downward. "I'm sorry I left without a note to you. I was frustrated and confused about everything. I needed to blow off steam."

Gabe appeared to accept the apology with a nod.

"Lydia loved the view at the top of the hill. She'd go there when she wanted to contemplate—said it cleared her mind and gave her a new attitude on whatever bothered her."

Melissa held the glass to her lips and took another sip. Her pain began to dull.

"You know, Gabe, I connected with that same feeling. To tell you the truth, I got scared. But also awed by the natural beauty I found. Deep down inside, I knew I was going to be okay."

"I recall Lydia referred to it as a magical place," he said.

Melissa nodded. "There is something magical about it. Sitting on the top of the cliff, watching the sunset — I felt a peacefulness. Like drifting free."

She took a deep breath at the thought of hearing her mom's voice. "When I was at the lowest point of being lost, I felt her presence." She gazed toward the window at the distant landscape.

The light from the table lamp cast a warm glow over Gabe's face. His smile eased into a somber expression. He didn't say anything.

Melissa bit her lip. "I thought a lot about what I've learned this week when I was alone there. Memories of things long forgotten. Discoveries I never knew. It all changed my perspective on some very long-held beliefs. I found a certainty, maybe you'd call it clarity, of the past. I found what I needed to do. What I needed to tell you."

"Melissa, you don't have to say …"

She interrupted him. "Yes, Gabe, please bear with me. Let me get it out."

He nodded and leaned back with hands folded in his lap.

She pressed her lips together and shook her head, struggling to find the words.

"I've caused myself a lot of misery. I've been bitter. My anger and depression, even my apathy, have affected my life. Not just with the relationship between me and Mom, but with other people too." Melissa lingered on the thought of the past years of loneliness. Disappointment with romantic relationships. Her pattern of pushing people away.

"This week has filled me with so many emotions I didn't expect. I've been rude to you. You don't deserve that, and I apologize."

He looked up and cleared his throat. "Look, Melissa, I want to apologize too ... for our argument. I said some harsh things."

She shook her head. "You said things I needed to hear. It made me think about my role in the estrangement." Her voice faltered. "I've allowed myself to be a victim, to see only what happened to me without thinking about what anyone else felt. I processed everything through my teenage mind and held onto it. I only saw what I believed was the truth and disregarded everything else." She managed a faint smile. "In my profession, that's labeled confirmation bias." Her hand stroked the sleeve of the robe. "I held onto my anger because it masked the grief of missing her."

Gabe raised his eyebrows.

"What?" Melissa said, "You look surprised."

Gabe straightened. "Well, I guess I am. I'm really glad you told me, though. It's just ..."

She watched him shift in his chair and waited. His voice softened to almost a whisper.

"I just wish she was here—you know—to hear you say that. It would have meant a lot to her. It could have changed a lot of things."

An ache swelled that hurt more than her bruises. For the first time, a wave of genuine sorrow coursed through her, leaving her arms and legs limp. She hung her head to hide a quivering chin. Her eyes burned with tears.

"Hey there, I'm sorry. Don't cry." Gabe stepped over to her and put his hand on her shoulder with a gentle touch. She wiped her tears with the back of her hand and sniffed.

"Here," Gabe said, reaching into his pocket. He pulled out a red bandanna and held it out toward her. She looked at him, then the hanky, and back to him.

"It's clean, really," he said with an amenable grin. A faint smile showed through her tears, then a half sob, half laugh burst out. Grasping the handkerchief, she dabbed her moistened cheeks.

"Everything will be okay. I think we both just need some rest. It's been quite a day," he said.

Melissa sniffed again and nodded in agreement.

"Do you need some help getting to your room?"

"No, I'm fine. I'll stay on the couch for a while."

He looked at her, his expression thoughtful. "You sure you're okay?"

"Of course, yes, I'm fine, Gabe. See you in the morning." She held a weak smile.

He switched off the light by his chair and stretched.

"Well then, it's bedtime for me. Come on, Doc." Gabe waved his hand, motioning to the dog to follow him upstairs. Doc raised his ears and looked at Gabe, then Melissa. He stood, turned in a half circle, and plopped by the couch.

Gabe shook his head and chuckled. "Looks like you've made a new friend."

"Are you talking to me or Doc?"

Gabe smiled. "Both, I reckon."

After Gabe left, she looked at Doc lying with his head between his paws and reached down to stroke his back. His fur still held the dampness from the evening's search and rescue.

"I guess I owe you a debt of thanks, too."

Doc snorted out a moist breath and closed his eyes.

Melissa leaned back, resting her head on the pillowed arm of the couch. The alcohol and pain relievers had kicked in. Her head floated in a comfortable haze. Soft cushions and the blanket swaddled her. Doc's steady breaths fell into a rhythm that lulled her into grogginess.

She blinked in slow motion, settling her blurry eyes upward. The smooth surface of the ceiling resembled an empty canvas ready to receive the brushstrokes of a new creation. She thought about her mother and wished for the chance to start over from a blank slate. Rebuild what was lost. There could be no reconciliation now, even if she wanted to. But what about forgiveness? The elusive acceptance of peace in her heart? Would it be possible?

She closed her eyes and drifted off to sleep.

Chapter 32

Saturday

In her dream, a metal door clanged shut. The clatter reverberated inside a hot, stifling tomb. Melissa stood alone, imprisoned, and blinded in the dark. A horizontal sliver of pallid illumination sliced through the inky blackness, drawing her toward it. The sliver grew larger, and Melissa floated through into a vacuous hole.

A single light bulb materialized and dangled overhead. Its sharp beam of light cast upon the skull of a genderless corpse. Shadows filled the hollow eye sockets. Desperate to turn away from the morbid sight, Melissa remained frozen, unable to redirect her eyes locked onto the decayed face.

"Where am I?" Melissa heard her own voice speak without feeling her mouth move.

Razor-thin lips, the color of mud, wriggled worm-like over the skull's decrepit features. Its mouth stretched wide and extinguished the meager light, swallowing it like liquid. Blackness returned. Barbed words spewed out, "I don't know. You brought yourself here."

The empty void pulled and twisted together to reshape itself. Mapped by unseen magnetic forces, particles formed like ink spilling on white paper. Bright red fluid splattered in a haphazard puzzle then rose in full dimension into a flame that flickered in slow motion. The remaining scorched remnant peeled away its charcoal edges to expose a huddled figure of a teenage girl curled into a fetal position. Melissa recognized herself, both as the observer and the observed.

Heaviness accumulated with each layer of sorrow stacked upon one another, each weight more unbearable than the last. The albatross bore down, seared into her skull, marched into her shoulders, and captured her breath. Tears burst forth in a torrent, not from her eyes, but purged from her gasping mouth, and filled a black river that surged below her feet. Water swirled in eddies of dark dances, rhythmic and mesmerizing.

She sensed but didn't see, another presence near her. "Come with me, Melissa." Her mother's voice whispered to her. The weight scattered and blew away. Her breath returned.

At once herself but also bonded with her mother in a symbiotic joining, Lydia's essence came to Melissa in telepathic waves. Thoughts only understood within emotional chords, strummed, and plucked. Time condensed to a moment but flowed eternal. Glimmers of past and future ran together. The lamp Melissa had seen in the studio rolled past on some invisible conveyor. A maternal giggle spilled out. The utterance of mirth her mother enjoyed whenever she made a joke.

Time faded like a delicate watercolor brushed across fresh snow. Weightlessness overtook Melissa again. The connection of the earthbound to the spirit of one no longer tethered to the corporal world. Nothing hidden or shadowed by the tenuous nature of mortal explanation.

Lydia's face appeared next to her and glowed with a shimmering warmth. Her hand reached out. A wispy caress brushed Melissa's cheek, no more than the weight of a feather, ephemeral and soothing. All anxiety bundled, compressed and packed away melted and disappeared. Her mother's kiss touched her, enveloped her, and surrounded her like the warmest blanket on the coldest night. Fragrant lilacs filled her senses, and rose petals showered around her like gentle snowflakes. No words were spoken, just the swelling of harmonics of heaven's angels. A rhapsody of forgiveness.

***

Melissa awoke from the dream with a start. The warm yellow hue of dawn filtered into the dark living room through the window blinds, spreading onto the couch, painting highlights and shadows across her blanket. A light flicked on in the kitchen and she heard Gabe's voice speaking something indecipherable in low tones. A sprinkling of dry dog food rattled in Doc's metal bowl. She raised herself to a sitting position and rubbed her eyes. The ice pack on her ankle had melted and had fallen onto the floor in the spot where Doc had been when she nodded off.

Gabe rounded the corner and stopped. "So, you slept on the couch all night?"

"Yeah, I guess I did." She said yawning.

"How do you feel?"

"Much better today." She rubbed her ankle. The swelling had all but disappeared. In fact, more than her ankle felt better. A refreshed outlook swept over her. Happiness. A feeling she had not encountered in a long time.

Daylight brightened the room when Gabe raised the window blinds. Dew sparkled on the green grass like tiny diamonds. Golden leaves on the trees in the yard fluttered in a soft breeze, catching and reflecting sunbeams.

He ducked back into the kitchen and returned with two coffee cups, holding one out for her. "Looks like it's going to be nice weather today," he said.

"Yes, It's a beautiful day. The coffee smells wonderful." She sat upright and accepted the cup from him, inhaling its steamy fragrance. Gabe seated himself in the chair across from her.

"I had a dream about her last night," Melissa said.

"Who? Your mom? He asked bringing the coffee to his lips.

She nodded. Her hand folded around the warm cup on the table.

"What did you dream?"

"I don't remember exactly. I just know how it made me feel ... frightened at first, but then, I don't know, like a burden lifted. Happy, peaceful, I guess is the best way to describe it."

Gabe smiled. "She always told me to pay attention to messages in dreams. Lydia was a believer that they help us figure things out when we can't make sense of our problems in the waking hours. She had a real sensitivity to ideas most people don't think about ... or think of as foolishness."

Melissa rubbed sleep from her eyes. "Did I ever tell you about the dream I had right after I got your letter?"

"No," he said, shaking his head with a quizzical look.

She lowered her gaze. "To tell you the truth, Gabe, I debated whether I should come here or not. I didn't want to dredge up the past. I'd worked too hard to pack it away. In fact, I more or less decided not to come ... until the next morning."

"After you had the dream?"

She nodded. "Whatever happened overnight ... it changed my mind. Perhaps it's been the culmination of everything that's occurred this week that brought me to a place I had to discover. Something I needed to find."

Gabe raised his eyebrows and gulped his coffee.

"Maybe it was the dream that influenced me. Or maybe just a feeling deep inside about something unresolved between Mom and I that needed to be healed."

"You made the right decision, Melissa. Whatever it was that convinced you, it was destined to be. I'm proud of you. That took courage."

She smiled, amused at his statement that he was proud of her.

"I don't remember much about the dream that convinced me to come to Iowa. But I do recall waking up early in the morning, 1:23 AM to be exact. It's strange. I remember that specific time," she said scratching her head.

Gabe stared at her. His mouth dropped open.

Melissa studied his face, confused by his apparent astonishment. "I know, it's weird that I remember the time, right?"

He stood without answering and looked toward a side table. "It's not that ... it's something else. Hang on a minute."

He walked to the table by the stairway, opened a drawer, and rummaged through a stack of papers. Retrieving an envelope, he pulled out its contents and scanned the sheet of paper. His mouth opened but didn't say anything. He walked back to where she sat and handed her the document.

Melissa took it from him. "This is the death certificate. So, what? I'm not following you."

He pointed to a section of the paper. "Look there."

"Date and Time of death," Melissa read. "Oct 7. 1:23 AM."

Chapter 33

Saturday Morning

Gabe disappeared upstairs after breakfast, and Melissa showered and dressed. She sat on the edge of the bed staring at the suitcase stuffed with clothing she had thrown into it the day before. The disarray of garments piled in a heap became a mirror of the frustration and anger she had packed away through her actions. Feelings and impressions tossed into accumulated chaos, destined to be jumbled and undiscovered. Grabbing the case, she dumped the contents onto the floor, spilling everything into a haphazard pile. One by one, she folded her belongings and repacked with care. One task accomplished for her flight back to San Francisco.

A few minutes later, Gabe called her name and she hobbled into the kitchen where he had just finished reading the paper.

"How are you feeling?" he asked.

"My ankle still feels tender, but surprisingly much better."

"It's your last day here. Is there anything you'd like to do?"

"Um, let me see. Probably not anything involving the woods."

He laughed. "Want to take a ride in the ATV around the farm? A farewell tour?"

"Sure, I can handle that."

The day burst fresh with sunshine brightening a deep blue sky as they climbed into the ATV. Doc clambered into the flatbed of the vehicle.

"Your run-about here is kind of fun. It reminds me of a souped-up golf cart," she said.

"Well, it sure came in handy last night," Gabe said with a chuckle.

Curled leaves fluttered in the cool air as the vehicle hummed through the yard. Doc balanced on all fours, jostled by crossing the bumpy ground. Melissa lifted her chin and took in a deep inhale. The crisp autumn breeze carried the scent of dew-moistened nature.

"I'm just going to check a few things in the parlor. Want to come?" Gabe said.

With morning tasks completed, the milking parlor stood vacant. He parked by the door.

"No, I may just take a short stroll. The weather is so nice. Don't worry, I'm not taking a hike today." She grinned.

Doc followed alongside her, stopping here and there to sniff the ground or to watch the chickens strutting about in their pen. The rooster approached them and cocked his feathered head, staring at her with a cold eye. Melissa stood tall with feet planted firmly in the dirt. "Shoo, Henry, go play with the hens!" She chuckled when he turned and strutted away.

Timid farm cats, who had scurried away from her only a week ago, now ventured close. Kittens frolicked around her and nuzzled against her legs. She picked up a calico and stroked the cat's head. It squeaked with a diminutive mew before wiggling in her arms with energetic twists. Melissa released her onto the ground. It bounded off, stopping in front of Doc, who towered above her. Doc cocked his head as the furry creature arched her back with raised hair and hissed at him.

The phone rang and she reached into her pocket to retrieve it.

"Hey, Melissa, how are you?"

The voice sounded far away, and it took her a second to process. "Hey, Dad. What a surprise. Where are you?"

"I'm in Venice. Drinking wine alone in the plaza." He sniffed with a dramatic inhale. "Francesca has left me."

"Really?" Melissa raised her eyebrows. "What happened?" From experience, she knew her dad spent the first several minutes of any conversation about himself or wife number three. She wasn't surprised when he jumped into the topic of his current problems.

"Ran off ... with a damn polo player. I'm miserable, Melissa. Everyone leaves me."

She waited until his torrent of lament subsided. "I'm really sorry to hear that, Dad."

"She was a greedy bitch, just like your mother."

Heat brewed in her cheeks, and she gritted her teeth. For her entire life she seldom, if ever, disputed anything her father said. His authoritarian tone carried such confidence that disagreements with him were better left unchallenged. But this time, his callous barb about her mom sparked defiance.

"Dad, I know you have your opinion, but I think you should show more respect for Mom. She wasn't perfect, but she was my mother. I believed the bad things you told me about her. I missed out on what could have been."

"You're being overly sensitive," he snapped back. "I just told you straight-out the way it was."

"Did she try to contact me after she left?"

"What? No, well, maybe. I don't remember. I just wanted to protect you!"

"Why didn't you tell me where she lived? You knew how sad I was after she left, how much I missed her."

"I didn't want you to be confused. She needed to be out of our lives. I didn't tell anyone about her whereabouts except for your busybody Aunt Irene, and that's only because she hounded me about it. I knew what was best for you. No contact. Your mother was an immoral person, and I didn't want her influence on you."

Melissa plopped down on an empty wooden crate and leaned back against the side of the barn, feeling the heat of rising frustration. "Maybe your motivation was to punish her more than to protect me. You fed me all your bitterness and I was too young and naive to believe anything else. You used me to get back at her ... and I paid the price. Now I realize the time I could have had with Mom was wasted."

"That's not true! I cared about your well-being, that's all. You're hysterical and overreacting. You made your own decisions, not me. You brought yourself here."

She took a deep breath. Speaking her thoughts out loud to him brought a sense of relief. Puzzle pieces assembled with a rush of clarity.

A long pause followed before his voice returned with a soothing tone. "Don't be angry with me. I'm sure her death is affecting your mood right now. I apologize." He slurred the word and it sounded like apola-size. "I hope you can forgive me."

Melissa rubbed her forehead, unsure if his sudden remorse was for his comments or his role in the estrangement.

"I think I've learned something about forgiveness lately." She took a deep breath hoping it would fill her cracking voice. "You're right about one thing. I did make my own decisions after I became an adult. I had the power to change the relationship and I didn't. I won't make the same mistake with you that I did with her."

He began to say something else, but she interrupted. "Listen, Dad, right now is not a good time to talk. I'm sorry about Francesca. I'll call you later." She touched the disconnect button and welcomed the release of emotion to wash over her.

***

After they returned to the house, Melissa headed for the couch with an iced tea in hand. Doc lapped water from his bowl in the kitchen with enthusiasm.

"I'll be upstairs," Gabe said. His expression looked pensive, but she dismissed his worried look as fatigue from last night's exertions.

"Okay, I may just close my eyes for a while," Melissa said, putting her feet up and stretching out full-length.

She must have dozed off because her attention rebounded when rustling noises upstairs disturbed the silence.

"Gabe?" Melissa called out, rising from her resting spot. She padded to the stairway.

"In the studio," Gabe's voice echoed back.

She ascended the steps with Doc following at her heels and entered the room.

"What are you doing?" Melissa asked, settling onto a chair. Doc lolled on the floor next to her.

Gabe sat at the desk sifting through papers.

"I'm just looking at her drawings."

He smiled, his expression absorbed in the images of flowers, barns, and kittens laid out before him on the desk.

"Look at this," he said extending one of the drawings toward Melissa.

She grasped the paper and studied it. The pencil sketch showed a portrait of three posed figures looking straight at the viewer. Melissa recognized herself as a child, about 6 years old, sitting on Lydia's lap. Gabe stood behind them. The resemblance between the young Gabe and Melissa's current features appeared with striking similarity.

Gabe pointed at the artwork. "She drew this from her imagination. I guess it was her what-if statement. A vision of an alternative reality."

Melissa sighed. "Do you ever wonder how everyone's life could have changed if different decisions were made?" She hesitated. "If I had made different decisions? So much wasted time making myself unhappy."

He stroked his chin. "Well, I guess we have to play along with fate and destiny the best we can. Our decisions can only be as good as what we see possible at the time."

"Is it okay if I keep this?" She placed the drawing back onto the desk.

He nodded. "Of course. You can have what you want from her artwork. I know she would have liked that." He fell silent for a moment. "There's something else she wanted you to have."

"What? Not another letter?"

"No," he smiled and shook his head.

Opening the bottom drawer of the desk, he pulled out a thick metal box, spun a combination lock, and raised the lid. Reaching inside, he retrieved a rectangular piece of light blue paper and handed it to her.

Her mouth dropped open as she read the cashier's check. The payment information was made out to Bearer for $20,000.00. She gripped the arm of the chair, dumbfounded.

"Lydia had a savings account and spent years putting away a little at a time from her teaching job," Gabe said. "She told me if you ever came back, she wanted you to have this. If you never showed up, it would be mine."

"Oh, my God, Gabe," Melissa brought her fingertips to her cheek. "I honestly never expected inheritance of any kind. I assumed she forgot about me the same way I forgot about her." She stared at the check, then at Gabe. "You could have kept this for yourself. I would have never known about it."

Gabe shook his head. "That's not what she wanted. It was important to her to mend the relationship with you as best she could. Saving money for you was something within her power to do."

"We should at least split this," she said raising the check toward him.

He shook his head. "I'm already a wealthy man. Maybe not so much bank account rich, but I have all I need." He waved his hand. "Consider it an investment from us toward your business."

"Thank you, Gabe. I don't know what to say ... just thank you." She rose and stepped beside his chair, wrapping her arms around his shoulders in a sideways hug, smelling his musty aftershave.

"This will always be your second home, Melissa," he said with tenderness. "I'm forever grateful for what Lydia and I made together."

He touched her hand on his shoulder, staring down at the drawing of the three of them. "Ever since I learned about your existence, I took comfort knowing I had a daughter. I understand you may not believe that right now, but I know it in my heart."

Her eyes brimmed with tears.

Chapter 34

Saturday Afternoon

Gray clouds filtered the overcast daylight through the farmhouse windows that chilly afternoon. Inside the farmhouse, warmth from a fireplace filled the living room carrying the scent of burning wood.

Gabe had left for the barn to check on some calves. Doc followed at his heels. With their absence, the usual activity of the household diminished to only the sounds of Melissa's occasional humming and the crackling of the fire. Her morning had been spent at the dining room table surrounded by sympathy cards. Nearly fifty people had sent condolences. Melissa offered to gather a list of contacts for Gabe and help with responses.

Her phone rang and displayed a familiar area code. She hesitated before answering, despite the ebullient tingle in her chest.

"Hi, Melissa, this is Jeremy."

"Hey, Jeremy. This is a surprise." She tempered her reaction, recalling the woman's voice who answered when she had phoned him earlier.

"I hope this is a good time to talk."

"Yes, of course."

"Did you call a couple of days ago?"

"Yes," she said, preparing for unpleasant news about a girlfriend or even a wife.

"I thought I'd call in response to the text you had sent,"

Melissa said. "I think the woman who answered said you were … unavailable."

"Oh, yes. That was my daughter."

"Your daughter?" Melissa said with surprise.

"Yeah, Katie. She told me later that morning a woman called but didn't leave her name. I didn't recognize the number right away. It took me a while to figure out it was you."

Melissa flushed with embarrassment about her haste to jump to conclusions. "Oh, yes, I think I was confused when a woman answered."

Jeremy chuckled. "Oh, I can see why you may have been surprised. Katie told me she answered because she thought the ringing would wake me up and she was right next to my phone in the dining room when you called."

Melissa blew out a breath and relaxed her tense shoulders.

"Katie and her husband had just popped into town for an overnight to surprise me. I'm usually an early riser, but we had been out to their favorite restaurant the evening before, and I slept in. Probably a few cocktails may have played a part in that too. I've slowed down a little since turning fifty-two."

Melissa's posture softened and relaxed into the dining room chair.

"I thought when you didn't return my texts, you weren't interested," he said. "I mean, maybe, I misread the signals about getting to know each other better."

A pleasant flutter welled up in her. "No, not at all. I'm looking forward to getting together."

"How about meeting for coffee when you get back?"

Melissa's smile spread across her face. "Yes, I'd like that. Coffee sounds good. I'll give you a call when I get home tomorrow."

***

After the visit with Jeremy, Melissa stood in the guest room, assessing her next task to finish organizing for the trip home. Clothes and toiletries fit in a snug arrangement inside the carry-on bag, including a book from her mother's bookshelf, Regionalism Art Movement and Grant Wood. However, the most precious cargo to take presented a problem. Her mother's unframed drawings.

She sat on the edge of the bed and shuffled through the artwork, choosing three works on paper that held the most meaning for her. She found a flat box and placed the first watercolor painting on the bottom —the landscape of black and white cows against a red barn. It embodied the place where she had suffered loss but also gained a new perspective on family and relationships. Next, she layered the charcoal drawing of herself as a teenager. Lydia had most certainly thought about her in happier times. Finally, the pencil drawing of her mother, Gabe, and herself as a child posed the most intriguing. The idea of twists of fate, decisions made, and coincidences made the sketch more than a simple portrait. A note to Gabe topped off the stack with shipping instructions to her apartment.

Two other small, framed pictures remained on the bedside table. She and Gabe had already agreed on plans for them.

Her purse held the airline confirmation, a billfold, and anti-anxiety chews. Holding the bottle of herbal gummies for a moment, she questioned her need for the remedy. Despite her emotional marathon of the past week, she had managed her anxiety without once depending on the additional aids. Unlike her arrival a week ago, she now held a sense of optimism.

The doorbell chimed a few minutes later. A visitor waited on the doorstep bundled in a quilted orange jacket and green stocking cap perched on her head, giving the impression of a ripe pumpkin. Her gloved hands clutched the handle of a pie carrier.

"Hi Sherry, come on in," Melissa smiled and stepped aside, motioning her to enter.

"I made a couple pies today and thought you and Gabe might

like one," Sherry said presenting the pie carrier to Melissa in a ceremonious gesture.

"Thanks, Sherry. You've been so kind to us this past week. I really appreciate your thoughtfulness. Have a seat and I'll bring some tea."

Sherry accepted a seat in a chair by the fireplace. Melissa took the pie into the kitchen. An apple aroma permeated through the cover of the plastic carrier.

"These are lovely flowers," Sherry said, leaning toward the bouquet of lilies on the end table and taking a deep inhale after Melissa returned to the guests.

"Yes," Melissa said, setting the two cups down on the coffee table. "One of the many flowers people sent to the funeral."

Sherry relaxed on the couch and took a sip of tea.

"Well, I just wanted to stop by and bring a pie to you and Gabe. Made from apples fresh from my yard." She beamed with pride. "I knew you'd be headin' home to the city soon and before you go, I wanted you to know it sure was nice meetin' you."

Melissa smiled at the neighbor. Sherry's face appeared almost childlike, eyes large behind her spectacles, cheeks blushed and plump, smooth skin despite being in her sixties.

"Thank you, Sherry," Melissa said. "Oh, wait, I have something for you too." She rose from the couch and left the room, reappearing a minute later from her bedroom holding the two small, framed pictures she had set aside.

"I knew you admired Mom's work, so I picked out drawings of flowers for you and your mom. Gabe and I thought you'd like them."

Sherry's mouth opened as she grasped the framed art, one in each hand. "Thank you, Melissa, and tell Gabe thank you too. I'll give Mom the picture of the daisies, but I want the one of the roses. I think roses are a gift from heaven itself." Her voice breathed a doleful sigh. "We will cherish these."

Sherry placed the frames on the table side-by-side and stared at them. A smile lit her face.

"I just gotta give you a hug," she said, rising with outstretched arms.

Melissa stood and met the woman's enthusiastic embrace with an awkward shoulder pat. The spontaneous act brought a smile to Melissa.

"I sure hope you can come back sometime, under better circumstances, of course. We don't get many visitors around here," Sherry said.

The idea of returning to the farm had not entered her mind. She had spent too much energy trying to run away from it.

"We'll see," Melissa said with a polite smile.

***

After Sherry left, Melissa wandered into the place that held the most presence of her mother. The studio. Clouds had cleared and gave way to afternoon sunshine. Natural light lingered inside the room with a diffused illumination. Dust particles suspended in its wake shone like tiny glistening snowflakes, creating a hushed sanctuary.

The faint smell of paint and pencil shavings clung in the air as she wandered through the room. She cozied up on a chair by the window and gazed out. Geese flew in formation over the rounded hills. Cattle grazed in a distant pasture. The steady and slow grace of nature awakened the realization of how much her life had changed in a matter of days. A reverence brewed inside her. Something deep emerged that had been shuttered away, necessary to be voiced, as if in a prayer.

"I'm so sorry, Mama," she said out loud. "I'm sorry for holding such bitterness for so long, pushing you away. Pushing everyone away. Now it's too late to tell you how much I regret that." She bit her lip and swallowed the lump growing in her throat. "Maybe all this has taught me something that I couldn't have learned otherwise. Maybe I just need to embrace people with all their faults. Accept our imperfect humanity. Recognize those unexplained magical moments as a miracle, a gift to be treasured, not analyzed."

Tears welled up in her eyes and her chest heaved. With her head cradled in her hands, she released the tears. After a few minutes, she looked up, wiping her moistened cheeks with her palms. Taking a deep breath, she held still. A perfumed scent carried in the air, unmistakable, recognizable. Roses. Her eyes widened as she scanned the room, searching for bouquets brought back from the funeral. No flowers existed within its boundaries. She breathed in once again, filling her lungs with the rich fragrance before it vanished as quickly as it manifested. She closed her eyes, recognizing the magic of the moment. "I love you too, Mom."

Chapter 35

Sunday Morning

Melissa and Gabe arrived just after sunrise Sunday morning at the Eastern Iowa Airport in Cedar Rapids. Gabe drove the Ford sedan up to the curb designated passenger drop-off and unloaded her bag from the trunk.

He walked around to the passenger side and opened the door. She gathered her purse and stepped out of the car.

He stretched out his arms. "Hug?"

Melissa smiled and wrapped her arms around him. His body felt warm and solid like his sturdiness could withstand life's upheavals. "Will you be okay?"

"Of course," he said with assurance.

She released her embrace and looked at him.

A flicker of sadness crossed his face before a smile returned. "Remember, you may have lost a mother, but gained a father."

Melissa smiled at his firm belief in his parentage. "I guess that means you may have lost your wife but gained a daughter."

She reached for his hand, looking into his eyes. "Thank you, Gabe. For everything."

His lips turned upward. "Take care ... and keep in touch, okay?"

"Yes, I will."

"Oh, I almost forgot," Gabe said. He retrieved a small packet from his coat pocket and handed it to her.

She laughed at the bundle of waxy orange blobs. "Cheese curds. I'll have the best treats of anybody on the plane."

***

Melissa waited in a seat at the departure gate for her plane to board when a text came in from an unfamiliar number. She opened the message. Her surprise turned to amazement as she read the message.

> Hi Melissa, this is Angela.
> I have a business proposal for you. We could use your marketing research expertise. Interested? I'd like to fly you to our Miami headquarters to talk details.

Melissa did not hesitate with her reply.

> Yes! Let's talk more when I get back.

The mechanized voice of the airline desk attendant squawked over the intercom announcing boarding. Waiting passengers sprang from their seats, gathering their bags. Melissa texted back.

> I'm about ready to board the plane back home. I'll call when I get back to San Francisco. Thank you, Angela.

She stowed her phone inside her purse and fell into the queue of travelers.

A young woman with pink hair stood in front of her and held a phone to her ear. Long earrings dangled over a tattoo of red hearts that ran along the side of her neck. A look of annoyance blanketed the face of the petite twenty-something.

"Stop being such a worrier, Mom. I'll see you in San Francisco this afternoon. What? I don't know." She hugged the phone to her ear, tapping her foot while the muffled voice on the other side rambled.

"Just Google places to park at the airport. I'm sure there are spots to pick up passengers. Yeah sure. Okay. Bye."

The woman deposited her phone into her midriff leather jacket pocket and glanced toward Melissa.

Melissa looked back at her with raised eyebrows.

"Ugh. Mothers can be such a pain in the ass," the woman said, rolling her eyes.

Melissa nodded.

"I know what you mean," Melissa said. "But there may come a day when you wish to hear her voice again and can't. Or recall a happy memory of time you spent together but she's not there to share it with you."

The fellow passenger cocked her head and studied Melissa.

"Have you ever asked her about experiences she had when she was your age? Something that changed her direction in life?"

The young woman smirked. "No. Why would I care about ancient history? What does it matter?"

Melissa shrugged. "Maybe it doesn't. But her history is intertwined with yours. Perhaps you can learn something about her that you had no idea about."

A frown mixed with confusion and insult crossed the woman's face.

"And you should do it before it's too late," Melissa said.

Chapter 36

One Year Later

Melissa and Jeremy turned off the gravel road and drove up the driveway to the farm. Gabe sat on the front porch on a wicker chair, Sherry seated beside him in an identical rocker. Doc lay at his feet.

Melissa emerged from the rented SUV's passenger side and waited as Jeremy met her and held her hand. The breeze wafted an earthy scent of cows. Leaves had just begun to turn colors and contrasted against the deep blue sky.

They walked together along the flagstone pathway toward the porch. Doc jumped up, barking.

"Hey, Doc! How's my good pup?" Melissa said in baby talk and bent downward with palms facing the approaching dog. Doc slackened his stance and lumbered next to her. His tail wagged and he licked her hand.

She ruffled his fur, stroking his head and neck. "He remembers me."

"Of course he does," Gabe said. "Who are you, again?"

Everyone chuckled. Gabe descended the steps and met her with outstretched arms, drawing her into an affectionate hug. Her cheek burrowed against his worn, cotton shirt that carried a comforting scent of something sweet and woodsy. She drew back to examine his face. His tanned skin, wrinkled from years of outdoor work, accentuated his glistening blue eyes behind his glasses. Creases framed his grin. Just as she remembered.

"I got your message you were coming. It's good to see you again," he said.

"You, too, Gabe."

She turned and put her hand on Jeremy's shoulder. "You remember me telling you about Jeremy Weaver?"

"Yes, nice to meet you at last," Gabe shook the man's hand with a vigorous motion. "Melissa has told me a lot about you," Gabe said.

"Hi, Sherry," Melissa waved to the neighbor standing on the front porch steps.

Sherry clasped her hands as if ready to applaud. "We're so happy you could come visit. Hard to believe it's been a year since you were here. It's nice you brought Jeremy along."

Jeremy approached Sherry standing on the porch.

"A pleasure to meet you, Sherry," he said with a smile.

"And you too," she said, casting an admiring look at him.

"I'll get lemonade for everyone," Sherry said and pivoted toward the front door.

Gabe motioned to the loveseat. "Rest a spell," he said, waving his hand.

Melissa relaxed into the cushion of the cozy settee. Jeremy sidled in beside her.

"How's it been going?" Gabe asked. "How's work?"

Melissa's eyes widened with enthusiasm. "It's great. I've been helping Angela coordinate her West Coast market research. I lead focus groups and website usability teams."

"That's wonderful. Lydia always said one day Angela would have a lot of influence on people's lives."

Melissa nodded. "Angela is great to work with. Brilliant, actually. I'm learning a lot from her."

Jeremy rested his arm around her shoulders. "Plus, you're busy with a new hobby." He turned from her and looked at Gabe. "I believe she became inspired by her trip here."

"Are you raising cows in your spare time?" Gabe asked with a grin.

Melissa threw her head back with a laugh. "No, I will leave the cows to you, Gabe. I'm taking photography lessons with a social group of hobbyists. I find it relaxing taking shots of landscapes, especially flowers, and nature."

"She's very talented, you know," Jeremy said.

Melissa nodded. "Well, I don't know about the talent part. I'm merely a dilettante.

But I'm finding a new, creative outlet that I enjoy. I think Mom's artwork motivated me to take a risk and discover new adventures."

"All that, and we still find time to be together," Jeremy said with a wink in her direction. Her cheeks warmed as she gazed back at him. She loved the way his eyes twinkled when he smiled.

Sherry returned with a tray holding four glasses of lemonade. After handing the beverages to everyone, she raised her glass in a toast. "To family and good friends." A chorus of unified voices filled the air and glasses clinked.

"Jeremy, would you like to see our vegetable garden I helped Gabe plant?" Sherry asked.

"Sure," he said, casting a glance at Melissa.

Melissa smiled with a slight nod. "You two go ahead."

"It's in the backyard," Sherry said, motioning for him to follow her. Doc raised his head but remained at Gabe's feet.

After Sherry and Jeremy rounded the corner of the house, Gabe turned to Melissa.

"Did you ever talk to Robert after we did the DNA test?"

Melissa nodded. "Yes, I talked to him right after we got results."

Several months ago, she and Gabe had agreed on the genetics test. Neither had been surprised by the results, identifying Gabe as her biological father. The moment her parentage had been revealed, a wave of unexpected emotion surged through her. A feeling of rebirth with fresh possibilities. The significance of being the same but somehow different. When she had phoned Gabe with the news, he had released a steady exhale, as if years of belief finally had been confirmed.

"What did Robert say?" Gabe asked.

"I thought he'd blow up, but he was quiet for a long time."

"He must have been pretty shocked."

Melissa shook her head. "Let's just say I was the one shocked."

"What do you mean?"

"Remember he remarried after he divorced Mom? To Tammy?"

Gabe nodded.

"Well, that marriage didn't last long, and he never talked much about his divorce from her. When I told him about the test results, he revealed his own secret.

"What was it?"

"He and Tammy wanted children but had trouble conceiving. When they went to a fertility specialist, doctors told him he was infertile."

Gabe leaned back. "Why didn't he tell you sooner?"

"That's what I asked him. The doctor said it was probably a condition since birth, but my dad wanted to believe the condition happened after I was born. Maybe due to some kind of toxic exposure in his construction business."

Gabe nodded. "How did you leave it?"

Melissa tucked her hair behind one ear. "He said he always believed I was his daughter, and always will be, despite the biology."

"I respect that," Gabe said. "He raised you. I don't mind sharing the Dad title with him."

Sherry and Jeremy returned and climbed the stairs of the porch. Jeremy carried a wicker basket full of red tomatoes.

"You and Sherry have a nice garden," Jeremy said to Gabe. "We have great markets in the city, but don't often get veggies freshly picked from the vine."

"Thanks," Gabe said. "It's always amazing to me what a tiny seed can produce."

"I'll take those inside and wash them, and make some BLTs," Sherry said, brushing the garden dirt from her hands. Jeremy handed her the basket and sat next to Melissa.

"Sounds delicious, Sherry. We'd love that," Melissa said. "Do you want any help?"

Sherry waved a dismissive hand. "Heavens, no, Honey. You all just relax and chat. Sandwiches will be ready in a jiffy." She disappeared through the front door.

"How long can you stay?" Gabe asked. "The guest room is all spruced up for you."

"Just a night or two here, then off again. We flew in, then rented the SUV to do a road trip around the upper Midwest area. It's so beautiful this time of year. We decided to take a week off work to do a scenic drive and take some photos. Of course, I wanted to show Jeremy the farm and meet you, too."

She leaned over to Jeremy and interlaced her fingers with his. Gabe cocked his head and stared at her left hand. A diamond ring circled her finger. "Any future plans you'd like to share?"

Melissa caught the innuendo and chuckled. "As a matter of fact, we do have some news. We're getting married next year."

Jeremy leaned in close and put his arm around her shoulders. "We wanted to tell you in person," he grinned.

Gabe's eyes widened. "Congrats! That's wonderful news."

"What about you?" Melissa's eyes rolled toward the front door.

"Sherry's a good friend. We keep company on occasion."

The screen door squeaked open, and Sherry appeared, wiping her hands on a towel, and announcing in a cheerful voice, "Lunch will be ready shortly."

Gabe stood and grinned. "Come on in and let's eat."

BEFORE IT'S TOO LATE

Printed in the USA
CPSIA information can be obtained
at www.ICGtesting.com
CBHW022117110724
11457CB00011B/516